Torn Apart

The Internment Diary of Mary Kobayashi

BY SUSAN AIHOSHI

Scholastic Canada Ltd.

Vancouver, British Columbia,
1941

Saturday, May 24, 1941

It's my twelfth birthday! Emma must have seen me looking at this diary on our last visit to Woodward's and knew I'd like it, even though most of our family think I'm just a tomboy. Kay is watching me writing this at the kitchen table. She's rolling her eyes at me like she can't believe I'll have anything interesting to write about. She's always teasing me — as if older sisters have some right to do that. But right now I don't care!

I've had such a great day. Maggie, Sachiko and Ellen came over this afternoon and gave me some wonderful presents — a pair of bobby socks, some pencils with my name stamped on them in gold (I'm using one of them now), and a set of sparkly barrettes. Instead of making *manjū* like she did for Harry's seventh birthday last month, Mama baked me a delicious birthday cake. We brought out the good china to serve it on and Kay poured us all tea from the silver tea set. I share my birthdate with Queen Victoria and today I, Mary Kobayashi, felt like royalty!

Even Geechan gave me a present — my own box of Maple Buds. He always gets annoyed when I raid the stash he keeps in his room. Last month, after I'd taken a couple from the box, hoping he wouldn't notice, he caught me red-handed! He looked really angry and chased me with a broom into the backyard, so I climbed the cherry tree, thinking I'd escape. But the branch I was holding onto broke off, and I fell to the ground! The next thing I knew, Geechan was putting a cold compress on the bump on my head. We all had a good laugh over that later.

But my very best present is that Mama and Papa agreed to let me go berry picking this summer when school is over. It's my first real job and will help pay for Girl Guide Camp in August. And I can save up for that new bicycle I want so much!

Sunday, May 25

I forgot to list all my presents yesterday. I'm not used to writing down everything that happens during a day, but hope I'll improve!

Kay gave me a *Glamour of Hollywood* magazine, which she'll enjoy more than I will. But it's fun seeing pictures of movie stars in their fancy clothes. Aunt Eiko dropped by and gave me an interesting book of fairy tales from around the world. I love reading so it was a thoughtful gift.

And I forgot to mention what Tad gave me! When he got home after work yesterday, he handed me a small parcel wrapped in brown paper. I opened it and inside was a real little camera! He'd bought it last week in Seattle when he drove there to get supplies for Cowan's Drugstore. Cowan's order wasn't ready, so Tad went into Kresge's to pass some time.

The camera was on sale for 99¢, a bargain gift for his favourite sister. I'm glad it wasn't expensive. We're not poor, but there are nine of us including Geechan.

Mike came home from work right after Tad and handed me a roll of film for the camera. Didn't say anything, but Mike's the strong, silent type, while Tad is always talking away. Kay says they're spoiled rotten being boys in a Japanese family — especially Tad because he's the oldest. But it was sure nice of them to give me such great presents.

Can't wait to use my camera at Guide Camp with Maggie and the gang later this summer. And what did Harry give me? A hug, which was as good a present as all the others.

Monday, May 26

Perfect weather yesterday, so after church my friends and I played tennis. Mrs. Franklin was sitting next door on her porch and scowled at us as we headed towards the courts. She's never been particularly friendly, but ever since her son Jack died two years ago, she's forever gloomy. At least she didn't lecture us about playing tennis on a Sunday!

Maggie and I played doubles against Ellen and Sachi and we won! We make a great team. I guess that's what comes of belonging to a tennis-loving family — well, Tad and Mike and me at least. Not Kay so much, and not Emma. Kay's more interested in boys, movie stars and clothes. And Emma, alias the brainy one, is just bent on getting her senior matric so she can become a nurse. She'd rather play piano than tennis any day.

Tuesday, May 27

Little brothers! Harry's airplane obsession is driving me crazy. Whenever he's outside, he's craning his neck trying to spot one. But I know what's got him extra wound up lately. North Vancouver had a big rehearsal for Air-Raid Precaution last week and brought in a low-flying bomber from Pat Bay. They even set pretend fires throughout the neighbourhood. Over a thousand people took part and the papers had lots of pictures. Harry couldn't get enough of the excitement, but he's too young to realize we have these drills because there really is a war going on.

At least most of it is far away in Europe. Still, people here are worried Japan might attack the west coast even though Canada and Japan aren't even at war. I guess that's why we had our first trial blackout here last Thursday. Harry and I were asleep when it happened so I asked my sisters what it was like, but they went to bed early along with everyone else in the house. They did say they made sure Rags was inside, the curtains were drawn tight and all the lights turned off by 10:00 sharp.

Wednesday, May 28

Couldn't write more last night because of my Girl Guide meeting. When Maggie, Ellen, Sachi and I arrived at All Saints' Church everyone was excited because the captains of our company, Miss McLeod and Miss Alston, mentioned the upcoming trip to Guide Camp this summer. Not only are Mama and Papa letting me go berry picking, but I can go to camp too. I'm so lucky!

When I got home, though, we had a depressing reminder about the war. Papa turned on the radio and we heard about the sinking of the German battleship the *Bismarck*. A few days ago — right on my birthday! — the *Bismarck* destroyed the Royal Navy's HMS *Hood*. Only three people survived. Now Britain has struck back. People keep getting killed and it's all so senseless. That's why I get so annoyed with Harry and his stupid bombers!

Thursday, May 29

Sometimes it's just so humiliating belonging to my family! Early this morning the milk wagon was on its usual rounds on our street. The gentle brown horse that pulls it happened to leave a dump of you-know-what right on the road between our house and the Muratas'.

Before I could even take the bottles from the milkman, Geechan was outside with his shovel and a bucket, collecting the manure for garden fertilizer.

Old Mr. Murata came out a bit later with *his* shovel and bucket and the two *ojiisans* were fighting over the poop! The milkman smiled at me and said he appreciated that he didn't need to clean up, but I was SO embarrassed!

Friday, May 30

Our grass-hockey team at Templeton Junior High played another team today and we won! Maggie and Ellen are such good fullbacks that they kept the other team from scoring. For once I didn't trip and get a nasty grass burn on my knees but Sachi crashed into another player and bruised her shin.

Finally started that book Aunt Eiko gave me. It's really good! My favourite fairy tale so far is the Japanese one, "The Peach Boy." I remember Mama telling it to me when I was little. One thing's different though. When Mama told the story, she began by saying, *"Mukashi, mukashi, ōmukashi,"* which sounds a lot better than "Once upon a time"!

Saturday, May 31

Even though it's Saturday, Mama still went to look after the subscriptions at the *Tairiku*, where she works part time. I guess the newspaper must go out, weekend or not. Papa went to Powell Street too, to have lunch at his men's club. He insists it's good making friends with all the businessmen, doctors, dentists and optometrists there, but Mama says he just likes talking. She gets annoyed because he drinks and smokes his pipe there!

But she knew he'd be leaving early today. He was meeting Tad, Mike and Geechan at the Powell Street Grounds this afternoon because the Asahi were playing. Our family (except Mama) is crazier for baseball than we are for tennis. Even *hakujin* admire the Asahi and call their style of play "brain ball." We don't have big, powerful sluggers, but we win by using strategy! Though Tad and Mike play on local clubs, I bet they'd love to be good enough to make the Asahi team.

Kay and Emma brought me and Harry to the game. Kay has a crush on one of the outfielders but *my* favourite player is Kaz Suga. He's a great hitter and he's a pitcher as well as a fielder, so he's multi-talented.

Today's game was a nail-biter. Angelus scored first. But the Asahi bunted in a run to tie. It stayed that way until the bottom of the ninth, when Ed Nakamura singled and then stole second. The winning run scored on a suicide squeeze play! Mama missed a great game!

Sunday, June 1

After church today, Papa convinced Mama to come with us to Stanley Park. She's always busy working, either at the newspaper or at her sewing, so I'm glad she took a break. Harry was excited we were going because he was sure he'd see a bomber flying over English Bay.

Before we left, I noticed Danny Franklin sitting with his parents on their porch. He hasn't been around since he joined the army in January. The Franklins must be glad he's back from his Edmonton regiment, especially Mrs. Franklin.

Danny looked so grown-up in his uniform. Tad went over to say hello. I'm sure Mike would have visited too, but he'd already left to play baseball.

Harry was anxious to leave, so Tad had to cut his conversation with Danny short. We piled into our car. Papa and Mama sat up front with Tad, while Emma, Harry, Geechan and I squeezed into the back. We even brought Rags — he doesn't take up much room. Kay stayed home to finish some of Mama's sewing. I think she's sweet on Danny and wanted to see him without the rest of us around!

Stanley Park is one of my favourite places in Vancouver. Even with all the people, you don't feel like you're in a big city. The seagulls were screeching over Coal Harbour and English Bay but Harry didn't spot a single plane! We drove past Lost Lagoon, then made our usual visit to the monument for the Japanese Canadian soldiers who fought and died in the Great War. Mama always says a prayer there for her uncle who was killed in France in 1918.

Even Geechan bows his head until she's finished.

After that Tad took us to see the famous Nine O'Clock Gun. We sometimes hear it on quiet evenings all the way back at Oxford Street! Then we drove to Prospect Point and walked around. Rags doesn't like being on his leash, but he behaved. We had great views of Lions Gate Bridge and the North Shore mountains. Next time, Mama said we should bring a *bentō* picnic — I'd like that.

Tuesday, June 3

Guide meeting tonight again. As the girls and I were heading out, I saw Danny saying goodbye to his parents, and Mrs. Franklin was crying. Danny got into a taxi and waved to us as he drove past.

I wonder why Mrs. Franklin wasn't upset when Danny enlisted at the start of the year. I guess she's proud that he's fighting for our country. At least she hasn't been as grumpy as usual. And now that Danny isn't around, Mrs. Franklin keeps calling one of us over to read her mail for her. She pretends she can't find her glasses or her eyes are tired. But we all know she doesn't know how to read!!

Wednesday, June 4

Tad surprised us at supper tonight. He said he's thinking of enlisting in the Canadian army. Did that ever start everyone talking!

Harry shouted "Hurray!" but Mike told Tad he was ridiculous trying to be like Danny. Tad explained that's not why he'd like to sign up — he really wants to fight for Canada to show how loyal Japanese Canadians are, and maybe enlisting will help us get the vote. Reading those advertisements in the papers gave him the idea (there was one in the *Sun* just this week — *Wanted! Men to Fight for Freedom!*), but speaking to Danny made up his mind. Being able to vote is something Papa and Mama have wanted for a long time. They supported the four Japanese Canadians chosen by our community to ask the government in Ottawa for the vote. That was five years ago, and Papa and Mama are still disappointed that nothing has changed.

Kay said how handsome Danny looks in his uniform. In my opinion, she places too much importance on a person's appearance. If Kay heard me say that, she'd be peeved with me, but I can write it here! Practical Emma told Tad he'd find it hard to enlist when we can't even get into so many other professions here in B.C. But she wished him luck!

Geechan began speaking to Tad in Japanese. I'm not sure, but he might have been saying that Tad shouldn't fight for Canada because he's really Japanese. Papa asked Tad if he really wants to enlist and Tad insists he does. Harry's excited by Tad's news but Mama didn't say a single word during the entire discussion.

When Tad kept talking about fighting for Canada, Geechan got up and left the room. I'm not sure if he was upset because Buddhists don't believe in violence, or if he really doesn't want Tad to join the Canadian army. Mama only sighed and we girls started doing the dishes. Diary, I don't want Tad to become a soldier. I'm worried he'll be hurt or, even worse, killed!

Thursday, June 5

Exams start next week. Math and Social Studies are on Monday, then Tuesday I have English Lit. Our gang is reviewing the poetry we learned earlier this year — those dreary English and Scottish poets are so BORING. Maggie wondered why we don't study some Canadian writers we heard about in Guides. Sachi, Ellen and I all agreed!

Friday, June 6

Grass-hockey practice tonight was cancelled because of exams next week — too bad! But it rained all evening, so I finished my book of fairy tales. Such interesting stories from all over the world! I can always study later.

Saturday, June 7

For weeks, Harry has been pestering us to take him to a Saturday afternoon children's matinee.

Yesterday he made such a fuss after supper that Mama and Papa finally agreed, but someone had to bring him. I said I'd do it on condition that my sisters would take me to something more grown-up later.

Maggie's little sister wanted to go too, so this afternoon we took Ida and Harry to the York Theatre over on Commercial Drive and stuffed ourselves with popcorn. The cartoon feature was *The Ugly Duckling*. Harry and Ida just loved it, but I hated how the other ducks picked on the one that didn't look or sound like the others — even its own mother! It was so UNFAIR. At least the duckling found a new family where it belonged, so the ending was happy.

Kay and Emma promised that when exams are finished, they'll take me to see *'Til We Meet Again* with Merle Oberon, one of Kay's favourite actresses. Kay's seen it already and says I'll need to bring lots of tissues!

Sunday, June 8

Should have spent more time studying this weekend, but it was too nice to stay inside! Maggie, Sachi and Ellen felt the same, so yesterday we went to Grandview Park and played tennis there. Afterwards we cooled our feet in the wading pool. On the way home we stopped for our first Revels of the year. Who can resist chocolate-coated ice cream bars on a stick, mmmmmm!

Kay and Emma were glued to their books when I got in, but Grades Eleven and Twelve are a lot tougher than Grade Seven. I studied tonight, maybe not enough for Math. Hope tomorrow's exams won't be too hard!

Monday, June 9

I think I did pretty well on the Math exam today but not so great on Social Studies — ugh! English Lit is tomorrow. Sachi came over tonight and we studied together. She's brainy like Emma, so I hope it rubs off!

Tuesday, June 10

A quiet Guide meeting tonight. Several of the girls didn't turn up, probably because of exams. Instead of grouping into patrols, our captains suggested we work on our individual badge goals. Ellen and Sachi want Knitter badges. Maggie's going for a Scribe one because her penmanship is so good. I'm useless at knitting so I'm trying for a Book Lover badge! I've already read four of the suggested books on the fiction list and just started number five. It's *A Sister to Evangeline* by Charles G.D. Roberts.

Thursday, June 12

Papa's been grumbling again about how anyone Japanese in B.C. must have an identity card. What does the RCMP want with our photos and thumb-prints anyway?

Tad once joked that Geechan's identity card is yellow because he's not naturalized, so he's part of the "yellow peril." Emma got really mad and gave Tad her famous "look." She told him not to say that again *ever*, even if he's kidding! Mama and Papa are naturalized and have pink cards. Tad, Mike, Kay and Emma were born here and their cards are white. Harry and I didn't have to get cards since we're both under sixteen, but Mama and Papa still had to give the Mounties our names, citizenship and birthdates!

Friday, June 13

It's Friday the thirteenth but I'm not supersti-tious! I wrote my last exam and I think I did fine. Played grass hockey with the girls tonight — it was good to run around after finishing my exams.

After supper, half a dozen of Mama's friends dropped in for their monthly get-together. They're so predictable. In spring and summer they practise flower arranging with flowers they bring from their gardens. In winter, they work on their sewing or knitting. And they gossip year round!

Papa was at his club tonight, Tad and Mike played tennis with friends, and Kay and Emma went to a movie. But I always stay in on these nights. My job is to keep Harry occupied and put him to bed at 8:30. At the end of the evening, I make green tea and serve it to the ladies before they go home.

Aunt Eiko came tonight too. She was pleased to hear how much I enjoyed my birthday book from her. I'm still reading *A Sister to Evangeline*.

Sunday, June 15

Ever since Tad said he wanted to join the army, I've been trying to understand his reasons and why it's so difficult for him to enlist. Now that exams are over, I asked Tad if he could tell me more. He gave me a bunch of clippings he's been saving from the *New Canadian*. Even though it's meant for Japanese Canadians, it's all in English, so I can read it. Not like the paper where Mama works, which only has a small English section. I guess that's what the *Issei* who've been here in Vancouver a long time want. I actually prefer reading the *New Canadian* over the English section of Mama's paper. It's much easier for us *Nisei*. I can write that here, but I wouldn't dare mention it in front of Mama!

I can't read Japanese at all. Mama, Papa and Geechan can, but not me. Mama might be disappointed, but I was SO glad to quit Japanese school after Grade Four. It was really hard spending the day at regular school and then going to Alexander Street for more classes in Japanese, instead of playing grass hockey or going to Girl Guides. Lucky Harry is the only one who's never gone to Japanese school. I guess Mama and Papa gave up after all the grumbling from the rest of us.

I'll read those articles Tad gave me later. I'm going out now to play tennis with the gang!

Tuesday, June 17

Tonight was our second-last Guide meeting before the summer break. Maggie, Sachi, Ellen and I walked over together. We were in our uniforms as usual, and Tad came home just as we were leaving. He joked, "Well, if it isn't the Three Musketeers and D'Artagnan!" Big brothers can be just as annoying as little ones! But then clever Maggie replied, "You're right Tad, we're all for one and one for all!"

The four of us love being Guides. Our company has girls from different parts of the city, so we meet new people and learn lots of interesting and useful things such as first aid or how to use a compass. And we play all sorts of games including an unusual one where we sit in a circle on the floor with our feet outstretched and pass a tennis ball from girl to girl, without using our hands. Our leaders say it teaches us co-operation, but we just find it makes us laugh!

Tonight we spent most of the time discussing the arrangements for Guide Camp later this summer. I can hardly wait!

Friday, June 20

Last grass hockey game of the year and our team won again. I scored two goals! My friends call me the best left-winger in the east end, which is very nice of them. I think Maggie and Ellen are the best fullbacks, and Sachi the best halfback!

Papa brought home treats from Cowan's tonight — Neilson's Burnt Almond chocolate bars. There was one for each of us, even Geechan. Harry says Papa has the best job in the world! I'm saving mine to share tomorrow with Maggie and the gang. I suppose silly Tad is right calling us Musketeers — we *are* all for one and one for all!

I've started reading those articles he gave me. They're so discouraging. Tad's going to have a hard time joining up, in spite of his good intentions. Every Japanese Canadian from B.C. who tried to enlist has failed so far. Emma's right — Tad has an uphill battle. But I'm proud of him for trying.

Saturday, June 21

Kay was fixing her hair this morning and asked me if the Lions were out. I rolled up the shade and could see the two North Shore mountains as clear as a bell. It's a pain sharing a bedroom with my sisters, but we do have the best view in fine weather.

Today was the first day of summer. To celebrate, the gang and I went to the Crystal Dairy Ice Cream Parlour. When we ordered our Double-Deckers, Len gave us all extra-large helpings as usual — guess it helps that he's Maggie's big brother. I don't even mind that he calls me Button Beak because of my short nose, but Maggie hates it when he calls her Eagle Beak because of her long one!

Sunday, June 22

After church I helped Geechan in our vegetable garden — all those rows of snow peas, green beans, cucumbers, eggplant and radishes. You'd think he'd be tired of being a gardener for rich *hakujin* families all those years, until Papa told him he was getting too old for that kind of hard work. But we all know Geechan still loves gardening. These days he only helps a few nearby families, like Sachi's just down the street and the Youngs over on Triumph. It saves him long streetcar rides and a lot of walking!

Our yards here at home are beautiful, thanks to Geechan. I can't decide whether I like the roses and flowering shrubs out front best, or the cherry and apple trees in the back. He and I weeded, then thinned out the rows of vegetables. At least it was Sunday, so there were no milk deliveries and I didn't have to help collect horse droppings!

Tuesday, June 24

Tonight was our last Guide meeting before we break for the summer. It will be different for me because of my job — I can't wait to head out to

Surrey to pick berries and make enough money for that new bicycle.

I'll miss my friends and seeing the usual girls from Guides, but it won't be long before we all leave for camp together. Miss McLeod gave us instructions for how to get there and a list of things we'll need to pack. We said our pledge and sang the Guide song one last time until we rendezvous at Wilson Creek in August. I'm writing this down quickly because I'm off to play tennis with the girls next!

Wednesday, June 25

This afternoon was so warm that our gang went swimming after school in the harbour down by Commissioner Street. Confession, diary: If our mothers found out, we'd be in big trouble for being around the log booms! But it felt so good to get wet and cool off.

Forgot to mention that last Sunday afternoon the girls and I saw *'Til We Meet Again* with Kay and Emma. Kay was right — it was a real tearjerker! It's a good thing I brought loads of tissues. Two lovers meet on a ship. They're both doomed to die but neither knows the other's fate. It's a ridiculous story but we all enjoyed it, in spite of the crying we did!

Thursday, June 26

Last day of school tomorrow — hurray! We girls all went to Crystal Dairy after school this afternoon because tomorrow there'll be a lineup a mile long!

I finally finished *A Sister to Evangeline*. It's so sad how the Acadians were forced to leave their homes and go into exile. At least the love story ended happily and Paul the soldier didn't get killed!

Friday, June 27

School's over! Papa and Mama are so proud that I made the Grade Seven honour roll. Maybe Kay will stop calling me a tomboy now! She passed all her exams and graduated from Britannia High. Tonight she's out celebrating with friends, but next week she starts dressmaking school. Mama thinks Kay will get more work with an official certificate.

Emma had the best marks of us all and was tops in her class. She's found a summer job at a factory packaging dried fruit, but is going back to Britannia for two more years to become a nurse.

I've no idea what I'll do when I finish school. My sisters still joke that I should become a hairdresser, seeing how neatly I trimmed the glass beads off the Tiffany lamp in the living room. Maybe I did, but I was only seven!

So now everyone except Harry will help support the family. And I'll do my part by earning money for my bicycle!

☙

Saturday, June 28

I've packed my suitcase already, because after church tomorrow Tad's driving me out to Surrey. I'm so excited! I'm staying with Mama's friends the Nakagawas on their berry farm. I must ask Mama to thank Gladys Nakagawa again for getting me the job next time Mama sees her at the newspaper.

I said goodbye to Maggie and the girls this afternoon. I'm a bit nervous because I've never slept anywhere else but here in good old Oxford Street. I don't want my parents to change their minds, so it's good having this diary to write down my thoughts and feelings. Rags knows I'm going away — he licked my face twice tonight. But while I was packing, Harry was fooling around with my new barrettes and broke one. I'm glad to get away from him for a while! He's such a *yancha-bōzu*.

Monday, July 7

I've been in Surrey over a week and I'm getting so tanned! I should have written here sooner, but I'm so tired at night, I just fall into bed and am sound asleep. Then I'm up early for another long day picking berries with the other people who come here to help. No days off, not even on Sundays, although some pickers take time off to go to church. I didn't go with them because they're Anglicans. I'll have to remember to say I've missed mass the next time I go to confession!

There are quite a few workers, some as old as Geechan. On weekends when she's not working at the *Tairiku*, Gladys helps pick too. Her three older brothers help Mr. Nakagawa load berries into their trucks every evening and deliver them to nearby markets. Mas, Ben and Joseph also do all the weeding and cultivating. Running a farm is hard work!

The first day Mrs. Nakagawa showed me how to pull strawberries off the plants quickly without squashing them. They smell so good, I can't help eating some as I pick. Whenever Mrs. Nakagawa's not picking berries herself, she cooks the meals for everyone.

Gladys — she must be around Kay's age — helps her mother with the cooking on weekends. I help by setting the table with bowls, plates and *ohashi*. Our meals are always Japanese — *onigiri* and vegetables at lunch, and *okazu* and pickles at supper. I miss Canadian food! We have toast at breakfast, though, with Mrs. Nakagawa's delicious strawberry jam. I'm exhausted at the end of the day but I don't mind. I always fall asleep smelling and dreaming of strawberries.

Sunday, July 20

The strawberries are finished now and we've switched to raspberries. They're harder to pick because of the prickly bushes!

Today I overheard Gladys talking to her mother

about registration. She'd brought a recent copy of the newspaper home, so I glanced through the English section. The Mounties are speeding up special registration of Japanese Canadians in B.C. My family registered back in April, but the Nakagawas have been too busy with the farm. Registration is mandatory now, so they'll have to find time to go to Vancouver somehow.

Working hard every day means I haven't had time to miss my family or Rags. I wonder if they miss me. Everyone here has been really nice. Gladys says that she enjoys having me around because she doesn't have any sisters. I like her a lot because she's more like Emma than Kay — she's not obsessed with clothes, hairstyles and movie stars!

Saturday, July 26

Tadaima! I'm home. It's good to be back. I really missed everyone — even Harry. He's not that annoying when I haven't seen him for a while. And Rags was so glad to see me, he ran around in circles!

This afternoon Mrs. Nakagawa handed me my earnings in an envelope to give to my parents. When Tad came to get me, she also gave me a big bowl of raspberries wrapped up in a tea-towel *furoshiki*. When we got home, Papa went straight to Crystal Dairy and came back with ice cream to eat with the berries — so good!

I have the BEST parents. Mama and Papa bought

my bicycle *before* I came home, in case someone else bought it before I could. It's the exact one I'd seen before in the Matsui brothers' bicycle shop — red with chrome fenders. I love it! Maggie's had a bike longer than me but hers is second-hand. After supper, she and I went riding all around Hastings Park and the Exhibition grounds. It won't be long before the fair opens again. I'd better go to bed now — I'm pooped!

Sunday, July 27

I love my bicycle! I really broke it in today. It's too bad Sachi and Ellen don't have bikes. Maggie and I rode all the way out to Lions Gate Bridge and back. We left early and took sandwiches. We got to the park just before noon, cycled to Second Beach and ate our lunch overlooking the water. Then we rode to Prospect Point and all the way up to Lions Gate Bridge. The mountains are wonderful when you're so close!

Geechan gave me a present yesterday to welcome me home. He made a little cage from thin strips of wood and there's a cricket inside! I've put it near the window, but Geechan said to keep it out of the sun or the cricket will die from the heat. I make sure it has food and water by putting a piece of wet lettuce inside the cage each day. I love hearing it chirp and sing but Kay and Emma think it's disgusting!

Monday, July 28

Got up before anyone else was awake to play tennis with the gang. I dressed quickly and crept out of the house. Sachi was waiting for me out front, then we ran to Pandora Park and met Maggie and Ellen there. The courts were empty because it was so early and Sachi kindly let us each try the new racquet she got for her birthday. We finally stopped playing because we were hungry and it was getting hot.

When I got home, Mama was busy sewing, so I made myself breakfast. We must have just had a milk delivery because there were three fresh bottles in the fridge. I used the cream floating on top of one to eat the last of the raspberries. Delicious!

Now I must make sure that I have everything on my list for Guide Camp. A Guide has to be prepared!

Tuesday, August 5

Guide Camp tomorrow! The weather has been good this week — hope it holds. Mama ironed my uniform and tie, so I'm packed and ready. Our company meets at the church early tomorrow morning with all our gear.

I'll be gone twelve days and can't wait to meet up with everyone. I put my bicycle in the garage and told Harry not to touch it! It's too bad I only had a short time to use it, but I'll be riding as soon as I'm back. Geechan said he'd look after my cricket. I'm not taking my diary with me because I bet anything I won't have time to write — I'll be too busy having fun!

Sunday, August 17

Back from Guide Camp! Only Mama, Emma and Rags were home when I returned this afternoon. Everyone else was at the Powell Grounds watching baseball. Rags was so excited to see me, he put his paws on my shirt. But since I was pretty grubby already, it didn't matter!

Am I glad to have indoor plumbing again. The first thing I did was to have a bath, Japanese style. I scrubbed off all the dirt and grime using a washcloth. Then I washed my hair in the basin before having a long soak in the tub. So much better than showering at camp! By the time I was done, everybody was back and cheerful because the Asahi won again.

It's good being home even though I had a ball at camp. I had so much to tell everyone, I didn't know where to start. Emma suggested I write it down and then I remembered my diary! I never did have time to write, so I'm glad I didn't bring it. But now I want to put down everything before I forget!

The day we left seems so long ago. But I'll always remember how the trip started — while I was on deck on the ferry, a seagull pooped on my tie! That challenged me to smile under difficulty like the Guide law says, but Sachi was a good sport and helped me clean up, so eventually I laughed with everyone else.

Then I was taken aback when I saw the tents at the campsite. I'd never slept outside before, so I thought of what Dorothy says in *The Wizard of Oz* — "Lions and tigers and bears, oh my!" But once we unpacked our things, I forgot my worries! Maggie and I shared the same tent with two other nice girls from our patrol, and Sachi and Ellen were right next door.

We ate lunch, then walked to the ocean and went swimming. Then we went bird watching and Maggie spotted a huge bald eagle on top of a dead pine tree! At supper each patrol had a specific chore, such as peeling vegetables, setting tables, clearing up or washing the dishes. We rotated chores so no one could complain. The worst camp inconvenience was having to use outhouses!

We had a bonfire every night, roasted marshmallows and sang until bedtime. My favourite songs were "Fire's Burning," "Home on the Range" and "Cockles and Mussels." We always ended with the Guide song.

Can't write any more — I'm out of practice and so tired. I'll finish tomorrow!

Monday, August 18

Slept in and woke up starving. I ate three pieces of toast and jam for breakfast! Geechan returned my cricket safe and sound. Now I can finish writing about camp.

After the bonfire we'd head to bed with our flashlights. I don't know about other tents, but in ours we talked for ages before we'd fall asleep! In the morning we washed with creek water, then gulped down our porridge to be ready for the day's activities. Each day one of the leaders gave a talk, then we hiked in the woods nearby or went swimming. We'd play tag or have sack races. We also learned some practical things about surviving in the wilderness, like how to start a fire without matches or how to signal if we're lost. I can't imagine ever using them here in Vancouver!

We even learned about finding food in the woods — it's called foraging. Miss Alston taught us about collecting fiddleheads (unopened ferns) in spring. In summer we can find wild berries. And in fall there are mushrooms, but we'd have to be careful because many kinds are poisonous. Afterwards we picked blackberries from the hedgerows. I collected the most in the fastest time because of picking raspberries at the Nakagawas' farm!

I took loads of pictures with my camera and can't wait until they're developed.

Tuesday, August 19

Tad, Mike and Papa were talking today in low voices. Kay and Emma were speaking quietly too and I recognized the phrase "registration card."

They must have been discussing what I'd seen in the papers — Japanese Canadians over the age of sixteen must now carry their registration cards *at all times*. The cards have people's photos and signatures on the front, and thumbprints and occupations on the back. They even list any "marks of identification." Mama's card reads, "small mole on right cheek." It's almost as if we are criminals!

Kay finished dressmaking school last week. After Labour Day she'll work at Maikawa's department store, doing alterations. Mama's really happy that she found a job so quickly.

I'm back riding again! Maggie and I rode all over the east end today. When we got tired we let Ellen and Sachi use our bikes. School starts soon, so we've got to make the most of our summer holiday while it lasts!

Monday, August 25

Went to Hastings Park this morning. Spent the whole day at the Exhibition until Harry got sick! Emma took the day off, so she, Kay, Harry and I got up early and walked to the park right after breakfast. Maggie and Ida joined us. We wanted to get there as soon as the fair opened. Papa gave us a whole dollar to spend!

First we went to the midway and tried to decide which rides to go on. Harry and Ida rode the carousel but Kay and Emma went on the Giant Dipper. Maggie and I wanted to go on the roller coaster too, but I wasn't tall enough. We took Harry and Ida on the ferris wheel instead and then to the Haunted House.

We had hot dogs for lunch and Harry ate cotton candy for dessert. Then we walked around the buildings and Harry munched on popcorn. I liked seeing the horses and cows, but Harry's and Ida's favourite was the Pure Foods building with free samples. He must have eaten too many, though, because when Emma suggested we get ice cream for a treat, Harry didn't want any!

The rest of us ate our cones but Harry rushed off to the restroom. When he came back he looked green, and my sisters quickly took him home. Maggie, Ida and I walked around a bit longer but Ida was tired, so we went home too. I was in time for supper but Harry was already in bed!

Tuesday, August 26

Harry's fine today. He says next time we visit the Ex he won't eat so many free samples!

Labour Day, Monday, September 1

Our entire family watched the Pacific Northwest baseball finals today, even Mama. There was a double-header so we brought a *bentō*. The Powell

Grounds were crowded but what an exciting atmosphere!

The Asahi played the Fife team from Washington. Each side has Japanese players but we all cheered for the Asahi because they're Canadians. Kaz Suga pitched both games — he's the best! We won twice and are champions for the fifth year in a row! Tad and Mike were over the moon and headed off to celebrate. The rest of us went home in a packed streetcar. When they got home later, Tad said he and Mike actually met some Asahi players in the New Pier Café! I took my camera to the game and used up the film, so now I can get it developed.

Kay starts at Maikawa's tomorrow and school starts too. Can't wait!

Tuesday, September 2

Back for my second year at Templeton. I've signed up for grass hockey and track and field again. The girls talked me into joining the school choir too, because we had so much fun singing at camp. But I'm really disappointed they're not in my class this year. Maggie and Sachi are together, but Ellen's in a different class like me.

There's an obnoxious boy named Billy Foster in my homeroom. Today he

Oh, I won't even write about what a pain he is. Better just to ignore him.

Wednesday, September 3

Our first choir practice tonight after school. I really wish one of the gang was in my class this year. Maggie and Sachi have Mr. Bell and Ellen has Miss Wright, but I have Mrs. Prentice. She's nice enough but hasn't noticed Billy pestering me. I hope he gets moved to another class. I'm trying to smile under difficulty, but it's hard!

Thursday, September 4

Grass hockey this year is on Thursdays. Thank goodness I'm with the gang again after class. I haven't told them about Billy Foster yet — we were too busy practising yesterday, after having the summer off.

I'm glad the weekend's coming and there won't be school. Maggie and I went for a long bike ride before supper tonight. I couldn't bring myself to tell her about my problem.

Sunday, September 7

I am NOT looking forward to school tomorrow. I know I should tell my friends about Billy Foster, but I don't even know where to start.

Monday, September 8

On my way to Latin class this morning, a school monitor stopped Billy in the hall because he was going up the down staircase! If he's found breaking student council rules again, he has to go to monitor court. I think he was following me, so I'm glad he was caught!

Latin's hard, but it helps being Catholic. Mass is all in Latin, so I know a few words already. Templeton's motto is *Pro Bono Omnium* — for the good of all! I wish Billy understood that.

Wednesday, September 10

Papa brought home my photos today. The camp ones are great and the baseball ones turned out well too. I'll add them to the album Geechan gave me last Christmas. It has quite a few pictures in it already. I'm waiting for a rainy evening to work on it — won't be long now.

Choir practice again tonight and Guide meetings start up again next week!

Friday, September 12

I LOATHE Billy Foster.

Sunday, September 14

On our way to tennis today, I broke down and asked Sachi if she ever got picked on at school because she's Japanese. She didn't answer at first, so I finally told her about Billy Foster. When Mrs. Prentice isn't looking, he pulls his eyelids down and whispers, "Hey, chop suey!" I'm not even Chinese! He makes me so mad and I don't know what to do. Then Sachi told me she'd been picked on at school every year until she came to Temp. I never knew! We hugged each other and Sachi said maybe I should tell Mrs. P. about Billy. And she said I could always count on her for moral support!

Monday, September 15

I'm glad I told Sachi about my problem. It hasn't changed anything (Billy managed to make another face at me this morning) but I feel better knowing she's on my side.

At least we have our Guide meeting tomorrow night. It's something to look forward to, which school definitely is NOT.

Thursday, September 18

Before anyone arrived this morning, I asked Mrs. Prentice if I could change desks. I said I couldn't see the blackboard because the girl in front of me is too tall. Mrs. P. looked at me curiously and I blushed, but she told me she'd see what she could do.

I'll have to say I lied when I go to confession! Is it still a lie when you say something to get yourself out of a predicament?

◯

Monday, September 22

I've changed seats with Gail Matthews! Her father is the manager at Crystal Dairy, so Billy wouldn't dare tease her!

What a relief. Sachi was so happy for me when I told her after school.

Wednesday, September 24

Choir practice again. It's fun, but not as much as singing around a campfire! Or sharing my camp photos with the other Guides at our meeting last night. And B.F. seems to be leaving me alone now, thank goodness.

Thursday, September 25

Steady rain today, so hockey practice was cancelled. When I got home from school, my cricket was dead. I'll bury it in the backyard tomorrow but I'm keeping the cage to use next summer. Harry's come down with a cold and went to bed early.

I put most of my photos in my album tonight after supper.

Saturday, September 27

Still raining last night and today. I've started reading *Jane Eyre*. I just hate how she's being picked on because she's an orphan!

Tuesday, September 30

Tad was excited today. A Japanese Canadian from B.C. has made it into the army! Tony Kato is from Duncan on the Island. Tad's convinced it's only a matter of time before more of us can enlist. He can't stop talking about it. Mike hopes Tad is right.

Friday, October 3

Finished *Jane Eyre*. What an ending — sad and happy at the same time! That's six books now towards my badge. I have to read a biography next but Maggie lent me *Lassie Come-Home*, so I started that tonight. Now Tad's calling me a bookworm!

Monday, October 6

It's hard avoiding the war when we're at school. Everyone at Templeton is organized into groups for war work. Grade Eight and Nine girls are in the Junior Red Cross Club doing sewing, knitting and even weaving. The boys are in the Training Corps and learn about airplanes (how Harry would love that!), boats, navigation, wartime science and industry, maps, air-raid precaution, first aid and signalling. The boys get taught all the interesting stuff! At least we learn some of those things in Guides.

The World Series is over. Tad and Mike are peeved that the Yankees beat the Dodgers again. They both say they always cheer for the underdog because of being Japanese Canadians in a *hakujin* world. I never thought of that!

Wednesday, October 8

Overcast and drizzly when I woke up. Couldn't see the Lions this morning. Kay and Emma started arguing over which of them owned a certain blouse. I kept out of it! This dreary weather is making us all cranky.

Choir again after school. We're already practising carols for Templeton's Christmas concert, even though it's over two months away.

Finished *Lassie Come-Home.* I'm so glad Lassie returned to her real home and was reunited with her master!

Thanksgiving Monday, October 13

Our big dinner was yesterday so Mama could spend today sewing. Papa went to work too, although just a half day and now he's home reading the papers.

The dining room table was crowded with Aunt Eiko here as well as our friends, the Hiranos. They've been coming to our holiday dinners ever since I can remember, so they're just like part of the family.

We used our good china and silverware, and Kay said grace before we had roast chicken, mashed potatoes, yams and the last green beans from our garden. Kay and Emma made two delicious pies from our own apples! I am very thankful for all my blessings.

Wednesday, October 15

I'm really discouraged again. Billy's back pestering me, this time in the hallway when we leave homeroom. He waits until no teachers or monitors are around, then walks past me slowly and pulls his eyelids down. Why must he be so horrid?

Thursday, October 16

After grass hockey today, Maggie asked if anything was bothering me. She's a good friend but it's hard explaining to her how much I hate being picked on just because I'm Japanese. Sachi understands what it's like, but I don't feel like talking about it even to her!

Saturday, October 18

Can't even read lately, I'm so upset about B.F. I'm writing my thoughts down here to see if it helps. I've been so miserable lately and can't hide it — even Kay asked if I was feeling all right. I didn't want to tell her about Billy, so I said the rainy weather was giving me a headache — another lie for confession!

Wednesday, October 22

Something happened today that made me forget my own troubles. Tad was really upset when he got home late tonight. He was returning from Seattle on another trip for Cowan's when a Mountie stopped him, asked all sorts of questions and demanded his registration card. It's a good thing Tad had it!

Then the officer wanted to see the documentation for everything Tad picked up in Seattle. Tad had copies of all the orders, plus the bills, so the officer finally let him go. Tad tried hard not to show his feelings until he got home. He said he'd never win an argument with a *hakujin,* especially a Mountie. And he also said if he joined the army, he'd need to exert self-discipline.

I just had an idea. Maybe that's what I need to deal with Billy Foster! Self-discipline, I mean. I must try harder not to show Billy my real feelings. He makes me so angry, though, I want to do something — *anything* — to make him leave me alone.

Thursday, October 23

Today I found out how wonderful my best friends are. Maggie and Ellen asked Sachi yesterday if she knew what's been bothering me lately, because they could see that I've been down in the dumps. So Sachi told them about Billy.

They all decided they *had* to do something to

help me. So the gang followed *him* in the hallway after lunch break today. He was concentrating so hard on catching me that he almost jumped when Maggie tapped him on the back. She said very smartly, "Billy Foster, it's not very nice of you to pick on Mary." Then Sachi came up in front of him and said, "Mary's our friend and we don't like you bothering her." And finally Ellen said, "Billy, you may think Mary's alone, but we're all looking out for her!"

My friends were so fearless. And Billy not only look stunned, he turned beet red. I'm sure he was mortified at being put in his place by GIRLS! And just then, Mrs. Prentice and Mr. Bell came walking by. Mr. Bell asked Billy if he was thinking of joining the grass hockey team. Billy turned even redder.

Friday, October 24

Another Japanese Canadian has joined the army! Harry Tanaka enlisted with the Royal Engineers in Regina. Maybe Tad really has a chance of getting in. I'm not sure if I want that to happen or not.

Grass hockey was cancelled yesterday. It's been too wet to play. After supper I helped Harry write to the *Province* newspaper so he can join the Tillicum Club for kids. They send you a secret password and print your name in the paper on your birthday. We put the letter in an envelope but the flap wouldn't stick. I asked Mama for some glue. She couldn't find any, so she took two grains of leftover rice and squashed them between the flap and the envelope. That worked perfectly!

Monday, October 27

Today two divisions of the Canadian army left Vancouver for Hong Kong to defend it against Japan. One is from Winnipeg and the other from Quebec. I'm happy Danny Franklin isn't with either!

It's good the army is helping Britain, but I'm worried that more people may be hurt or killed. I heard Papa telling Tad that he thinks Japan is too aggressive for its own good. I'm glad Papa doesn't support Japan.

Friday, October 31

Maggie and I took Harry and Ida trick or treating tonight. Mama made Harry a ghost costume from an old tablecloth and Ida wore a blue gingham smock with a white blouse to be Dorothy from *The Wizard of Oz*. Maggie put Ida's hair in pigtails and we took Rags along for Toto. He's the wrong colour but the only dog available! It was so wet out that we didn't visit many houses before calling it quits.

Tuesday, November 4

I haven't written in here for a while because I found a really interesting book in the school library last week. It's called *A Daughter of the Samurai* by Etsu Sugimoto. She was born in Japan, raised as a Buddhist, but came to the United States to get married. The book's on the suggested reading list for my Guide badge, so I've spent all weekend reading it and I'm still not done.

What a contrast between Mrs. Sugimoto's life in Japan and then in America. I could never live in Japan — the women must be so obedient to the men. I bet Mama's glad that she doesn't live there anymore either!

Wednesday, November 5

In English class, we're studying what Miss Wright calls the great romantic poets — Wordsworth, Shelley and Sir Walter Scott. I've got to memorize some stanzas from "The Rime of the Ancient Mariner" by Samuel Taylor Coleridge — ugh! And I'm supposed to read either an entire narrative poem or four lyric poems for my Guide badge. That's going to be a real challenge.

It's been almost two weeks since my friends told off Billy and he's left me blissfully alone!

Thursday, November 6

Harry received his secret password from the Tillicum Club today, along with a little totem pole he's wearing on a piece of string around his neck. He runs around the house saying, "Klahowya!" If that's the secret password, it isn't secret anymore!

The rain held off this afternoon long enough for us to get in our grass-hockey game. The season will end soon, though. It's a good thing I like reading so much.

Monday, November 10

Finally finished *A Daughter of the Samurai.* Now Kay's calling me a bookworm! I learned a lot about Japan, but that way of life seems so strange.

Don't know what to read next. Kay won't lend me her copy of *Gone With the Wind* — she says it's too racy for me!

Tuesday, November 11

It's Remembrance Day. Muriel Bishop recited "In Flanders Fields" at the assembly this morning. Afterwards we had a minute of silence at eleven o'clock.

Mama went to Stanley Park for the service with the Japanese Canadian veterans. She said there was a good turnout at the memorial, and that it was nice seeing the men from the same battalion as her uncle. They must be getting really old, but Mama says they still remember Uncle Hiko almost twenty-five years later!

Thursday, November 20

Rain again today. Harry's started coughing too. Hope he's not getting sick.

Just realized that it's been a whole month since the gang told Billy off and he's left me alone!

Friday, November 28

Harry had a fever, so Mama kept him home from school today and didn't go out to work. She almost cancelled tea night, but Harry's temperature was back to normal when I got home from school. Her friends are here now, so Kay and Emma stayed in to look after Harry. Emma just checked and he's sound asleep. I hope he's better soon.

Thursday, December 4

Harry was well enough to go to school today.

Sunday, December 7

Today began as a beautiful sunny day. We all went to mass, except Geechan, who went to his Buddhist church. Father Benedict asked us to pray for an end to this war once more. But after we got home, Papa turned on the radio and we learned something dreadful has happened.

The announcer said that Japan had bombed America's military base at Pearl Harbor in Hawaii early this morning. American battleships were sunk or damaged and many airplanes destroyed. Even worse, hundreds of people were killed or injured. I felt terrible hearing this and Mama and Papa looked really unhappy.

The phone rang right after we heard the news. Mr. Kusumi wanted Mama to come in to the newspaper early tomorrow to help prepare a special issue about Japan's surprise attack.

We were all quiet at supper tonight. Except for Harry, who was being his usual *yancha* self, pretending to fly his toy airplane as a bomber. I asked him to stop because I kept thinking about the real people who died. He said I was picking on him, so I called him thoughtless. Mama scolded me, saying Harry is too young to understand, but she took his plane away. He sulked until supper was over. Mike says this action of Japan's won't be good for us. He's probably right.

The day ended so differently from how it began. The war has finally become real in a way it never was before.

Monday, December 8

Canada is at war with Japan!

I'm so confused and scared. Maybe writing about it will help.

The papers arrived this morning and all the headlines were about Pearl Harbor. The attack killed more people than I first thought — THOUSANDS have died. And many more have been wounded. I feel sick thinking about it.

At Templeton everyone was talking about the attack, expecting President Roosevelt to declare war against Japan any moment. Then this afternoon we learned that Canada already has. As soon as Mrs. Prentice made the announcement, Billy and some other boys cheered. Mrs. P. asked them to be quiet. She said we must remember that the students of Japanese background in this school are *Canadian* and shouldn't be confused with the Japanese in Japan. But some of the kids kept looking at me. Billy was actually glaring.

Then when I got back from school, both Mama and Papa were at home! The government has closed all the Japanese newspapers! Only one can still publish — and it's not Mama's paper, it's the *New Canadian*. Mike muttered that it's the only one the government can read because it's all English! Every Japanese-language school in B.C. has been closed down too.

Papa came home early because Mr. Cowan told him to take a few days off. When I asked why, Papa would only say it was just until things settle down. We found out the real reason when Tad came home later.

This morning some *hakujin* customers complained to Mr. Cowan about Papa. They actually believed he has something to do with the Japanese who attacked Pearl Harbor. That is so *crazy!* Papa was born in Japan but he's Canadian. We all consider ourselves one hundred percent Canadian, except perhaps Geechan, and even he's lived in Canada over twenty-five years!

Tad's able to keep working at Cowan's because he's either in the stockroom or out doing deliveries, so no one pays him much attention. He says it helps not having a Japanese accent! But Mr. Cowan was very busy today without Papa around.

Later

On the eight o'clock news, we listened to President Roosevelt's speech declaring war on Japan at last. He called December 7 "a date which will live in infamy." Then the announcer said the Canadian navy has seized all the fishing boats belonging to Japanese Canadians in B.C. — twelve hundred in total! Papa shook his head in disbelief.

And the last strange thing is blackout. This is not practice anymore. Tonight all our windows must be covered with curtains or heavy blankets so not a sliver of light can show. People are terrified that Japan could attack right here in Vancouver and they don't want any lights to provide targets!

Tuesday, December 9

Last night I woke up and heard Harry crying, scared by the total darkness everywhere. Mike brought him upstairs and put him in Mama and Papa's bed, but I couldn't get back to sleep right away. I don't think anyone slept very well last night.

And there's nothing but bad news in the papers this morning. President Roosevelt's speech is printed in full. Yesterday Japan attacked Hong Kong as well as the Philippines and destroyed many more American planes.

Later

Since the Pearl Harbor attack, we're expected to try harder to meet Templeton's War Saving Stamps targets. The girls are supposed to do more for the Red Cross, so I agreed to knit some socks even though I'm bad at it. Knitting doesn't make me feel any better about this war, but Sachi says it makes her feel useful.

It's so peculiar having *both* Mama and Papa here after school. Mama at least keeps busy sewing, but poor Papa doesn't know what to do. He can't go to his club anymore because it's been closed. The newspapers are all scattered across the dining-room table and he reads them over and over. Mama says he listens to every news report on different radio stations throughout the day. I hope he's back at work soon!

Miss Alston called to say Guide meetings are cancelled this month. We had only one more before Christmas break, but I'm still disappointed.

And when he was coming home tonight, Tad

almost hit another car. It's hard enough seeing in the gloom, but now all vehicles must put blackout shields on their lights. Tad's lucky he can still drive because making drugstore deliveries is considered important. Cars and trucks may soon be allowed on the road only for essential purposes. People will have to get special permits for everything else. Just what we need, Tad said, more permits!

Wednesday, December 10

Today was election day in Vancouver but the only Japanese allowed to vote were the veterans from the Great War. Only one other Japanese person, a Mr. Sugiyama, was able to vote here today, because he's a naturalized *British* subject.

That's ridiculous! Someone from another country can vote, but naturalized Canadians like Papa and Mama or those born here like Tad can't! Mike says that's why the government won't let Japanese Canadians enlist – they'd have to give them the vote. I wish we *could* vote, if only to get rid of that awful alderman, Halford Wilson.

For years, Papa and Mama have been saying what a horrible man Mr. Wilson is. He thinks anyone with Japanese ancestry is a menace! He tried to ban us from getting business licences and he wants all Orientals to live and work in just one part of the city. Once I even heard Mama call him *baka* – she never uses that word for anyone else.

Later

Went to choir practice with Maggie and Sachi. Just made it home before it was totally dark. Blackout's on again tonight — it's so depressing. I've done all my homework and am going to bed!

Thursday, December 11

The United States has declared war on Germany and Italy. I feel like the world has gone crazy.

But one good thing happened today. The milkman was delivering our bottles as I was about to leave for school this morning. He asked me to tell my parents he's sorry some people are so negative about the Japanese here in Vancouver. He said they're his best customers and the nicest people! I thanked him and ran in to tell Mama and Papa. That cheered them up for a little while at least.

Friday, December 12

Papa went back to work today! Mr. Cowan couldn't spare him any longer. Now that winter's almost here, lots of people are sick with colds and flu. I hope that Harry doesn't catch anything. Papa doesn't give out any medicines because no Japanese Canadians in B.C. can get a pharmacist's licence, but Mr. Cowan says he really needs Papa back to take orders and help prepare the prescriptions. Which reminds me, Papa made us start taking a daily dose of Wampole's Vitamin Tonic this morning — ugh! But Maggie's mother always gives her cod liver oil — double ugh! — so I shouldn't complain.

After supper I read the *New Canadian*. The news is all discouraging. Eighteen hundred fishermen are out of work along with fifty newspaper workers (and that includes Mama!) and all the Japanese schoolteachers. Section hands and redcaps were dismissed from the CPR, bellhops fired from the hotels, sawmill hands laid off. Somebody set fire to a rooming house on Alexander Street and smashed windows in some West End and Grandview shops. All because the workers or business owners are Japanese!

It makes me feel sick. How can anybody do such dreadful things? How will people who have lost their jobs pay their bills and buy food for their families? We've heard about some awful things happening to Jewish people in Germany because of the Nazis, like being confined to just certain areas in the cities. That sounded so far away until now. I keep telling myself at least we live in Canada and those things can't possibly happen to us.

Sunday, December 14

Father Benedict's sermon about Pearl Harbor this morning made me cranky, but I forgot about it once I got home. Spent the entire weekend helping with the Christmas baking. It kept my mind off

worrying! The girls even came over to help yesterday because Kay was working. Emma made plum
pudding, while Mama did the Christmas cakes.
Maggie and Sachi mixed cookie dough while Ellen
and I rolled it and cut out the shapes. Harry helped
us decorate them. We saved up our sugar for this,
but at least it hasn't been rationed like in England.
The house smelled so good!

Tuesday, December 16

We had a drill at school today. Mrs. P. gave
out gas masks and showed how to use them. We
pretended to study until a siren went off. Then we
put on our masks and had to evacuate the building. Once everyone had them on, we realized how
bizarre we looked — even Mrs. Prentice!

I can't wait for the holidays. I haven't enjoyed
school since Pearl Harbor, and Billy's back making
faces at me. At least the teachers have acted normal,
and the other *hakujin* students haven't been nasty, but
all the Japanese kids at Temp are feeling uncomfortable. I never thought anyone would ever confuse us
with the Japanese in Japan, but I was wrong. Sachi says
there's a cloud of suspicion over us now. She's right.

Wednesday, December 17

Mama went Christmas shopping on Powell Street
today. She usually visits Woodward's once a month

but since Pearl Harbor she's been avoiding stores like that. When I asked why and she explained, I got upset again. When Mama's friend Mrs. Oda was in Woodward's last week, a salesclerk told her to go back to Japan where she belonged! Mrs. Oda was so shocked, she left the store without her shopping. Mama says there are good buys at Shibuya's and she'll check out Furuya's and Maikawa's next week.

The *New Canadian* is publishing free ads for people in our community looking for help or for work. That makes me feel better about all those who lost their jobs. I hope the Japanese stores will need extra help if everyone avoids the *hakujin* shops this Christmas.

I helped Harry write his letter to Santa Claus tonight. We're going to mail it tomorrow.

Thursday, December 18

Not a good day. Mama was crying but tried to hide it from us. Mrs. Shimura told Mama that when her son was in Stanley Park yesterday, he noticed the light on the memorial to Japanese Canadians soldiers had been turned off! Diary, I admit I used to get tired of Mama telling us about how Great Uncle fought and died for Canada. But this is really rotten.

Papa and Geechan were talking in Japanese after supper tonight. Papa was saying the government now wants Geechan to report to the RCMP every month because he never became naturalized.

Geechan was unhappy about this and Papa was having a hard time explaining. I think he was asking Geechan to be patient and put up with this situation. I feel bad for them both.

Friday, December 19

Templeton's Christmas concert was this afternoon — it was great. All our practice paid off! My favourite songs were "I Saw Three Ships," "It Came Upon a Midnight Clear" and "Deck the Halls." We ended with a non-Christmas song and everyone cheered our hit parade special — "Chattanooga Choo Choo!" It made a good start for the weekend!

Saturday, December 20

Emma and I did our Christmas shopping today. I finished most of mine, although it was hard having Emma in the stores with me. But I managed!

It was odd not shopping in Woodward's. But my sisters and I decided if their salespeople are rude to a kind person like Mrs. Oda, we'd shop on Powell Street instead. There were *nihonjin* everywhere. I never knew there were so many of us! But the clerks spoke perfectly good English. And why wouldn't they, since most were born here! Like the girl in Maikawa's who thanked us for our business and gave us free candy canes. I'm saving mine for Harry.

Tad got excited reading the *New Canadian* tonight. There was a photo of Corporal Jack Nakamoto. He travelled east three years ago and finally joined the Royal Canadian Engineers of Quebec last year. Tad said that maybe he should go to Quebec to get into the army. I must have looked upset because he said he was just joking.

Blackout's been lifted. It would have been too dismal at Christmas! Tonight we put up some cedar boughs and holly inside the house. It's starting to look cheery. Harry has started searching for presents, so I'll be careful where I hide mine!

Sunday, December 21

Harry couldn't sit still in church today because Tad and Mike were taking him to get our Christmas tree right afterwards. The rest of us went home to clear space in the living room. The boys came back with a big fir tree and now the whole house smells even more Christmassy.

We spent all afternoon decorating. Papa got out our first set of electric Christmas lights he bought last year and put them on the tree. Kay and Emma made popcorn and strung it with thread to make garlands. Harry ate so much we only ended up with two strands! Then we added the ornaments. I love the old European ones Mama and Papa have had since before Tad was born. I made a few little *origami* cranes for the final touch. Geechan taught me how to make them a few years ago and now I can do it pretty quickly. The tree looks perfect!

I read an article tonight saying sales of bicycles, wagons, ice skates and roller skates will soon be banned because Canada needs the metal for the war effort. People should buy toys now while supplies last. I hope Harry gets his ice skates from Santa this Christmas!

Tuesday, December 23

The holidays are finally here! Maggie, Ellen, Sachi and I ran all the way home from school. The girls came in for Ovaltine and admired our Christmas tree. Maggie really likes the *origami* cranes I made. I said I'd come by early tomorrow to see her tree before her family has their big holiday meal at lunchtime, the way Swedish people traditionally do.

Wednesday, December 24

I took Harry with me when I went to Maggie's this morning because now that school's out, Mama said he's being *urusai.* I gave Maggie some pretty *origami* paper and promised to show her how to make a crane later. She gave me a cute little straw goat for our tree. Mrs. Svendson also gave me some gingerbread cookies for our family. We wished Maggie's family a Merry Christmas and went home.

That darn Harry ate nearly all the cookies before I stopped him!

I stayed out of the living room when the news came on tonight and didn't look at the papers either. I'm not spoiling Christmas Eve with bad news!

Thursday, December 25

Christmas Day. I'm sitting on my bed writing and sorting out my thoughts. I usually love Christmas, but today's been very different.

We all got up early and opened our presents around the tree. But the only one who seemed to be enjoying himself was Harry. The rest of us were quiet, even Kay. I suppose we were thinking about what could happen in the coming weeks. Papa's been more positive about things since he went back to work, but Mama, Mike and Geechan aren't. Tad still wants to enlist, but Pearl Harbor is a huge setback for him.

We did get some nice gifts. Mama made everyone clothes again and Santa brought Harry his ice skates and warm slippers for Geechan. Harry also got a Meccano set and I gave him an airplane jigsaw puzzle.

At mass this morning, the church was full and people wished each other Merry Christmas, but I thought the spirit behind the words was missing. I can't really explain why. Father Benedict talked about the feeling of hope we have with the birth of the Christ child. But instead of being hopeful, I was sad. I can't imagine what Christmas must be like for those fishermen's families and the other Japanese here who lost their jobs through no fault of their own. Or the families of the people who died at Pearl Harbor. I was glad to get home.

Supper was the best part of the day. Aunt Eiko came around noon, then the Hiranos arrived about four o'clock. An hour later, the twelve of us crowded around the table but we're used to it. We had Christmas crackers and everyone wore their silly paper hats, including Geechan. Emma even let Harry carefully set a match to the brandy she poured over the plum pudding. We turned out the lights and she brought it in to cheers all around.

Later

The Japanese have taken Hong Kong!

After supper we put on the radio and heard the terrible news. Nearly two thousand Canadian soldiers have surrendered! Those men who were sent off to cheers from the city back in October are now prisoners. I'm so relieved Tad wasn't able to enlist. He might have ended up fighting there and been captured. Would Japanese soldiers have found it strange if a Japanese *Canadian* soldier was fighting against them? I am also very thankful that Danny Franklin wasn't sent to Hong Kong.

But now I'm really worried about what might

happen because of this awful turn of events. Before they went visiting some friends tonight, Tad and Mike were whispering in the foyer — they BOTH think there will be terrible repercussions for us.

I felt a bit better listening to the king's Christmas message after the news. He talked about the family circle. At least my family is all together here, safe in our home!

Friday, December 26

It's appalling what the papers say happened in Hong Kong before the Canadian soldiers surrendered. On Christmas Eve, the Japanese attacked a hospital and killed doctors, nurses and even the wounded soldiers in their beds. It's too wretched to think about! I'm so afraid that *hakujin* like Billy Foster will see this as a reason to hate Japanese Canadians more than ever.

Saturday, December 27

Today Mama had us all cleaning up the house for New Year's. At least I don't have time to think about the gruesome news coming out of Hong Kong. We girls were washing, cleaning, ironing, dusting and polishing. We put Rags outside while we worked. The boys had to move furniture, then roll up the rugs and beat them outside. Even Harry had to help. Tad and Mike were washing windows.

Papa and Geechan got rid of all the old newspapers and magazines.

After supper we listened to Artie Shaw on the radio but Glenn Miller is still my favourite. Harry wanted to listen to *The Lone Ranger* but he was outnumbered! At least tomorrow is Sunday so we shouldn't have to work so hard.

Monday, December 29

Mama went to Powell Street for the special ingredients she needs for the New Year's dishes she's making. Kay and Emma went too but I stayed home with Harry. Maggie and Ida came over, so the four of us played Parcheesi and Snakes and Ladders. Harry and I also taught Maggie and Ida how to play *Jan-Ken-Pon*. It was fun!

Last night I asked Tad and Mike if I could play their new records. They agreed as long as I promised not to scratch them. Maggie loves Glenn Miller's music as much as I do! Our new favourite song is "Elmer's Tune."

Tuesday, December 30

Today's headlines are about "conscription." Papa says that's what *making* people join the army or navy is called. Next spring Canadians can vote on what our government should do. Too bad *we* can't vote!

Canada needs soldiers more than ever, so Tad took time off work today and went to the recruiting office with his friend George Fujino. They were told to contact Ottawa directly to enlist. I overheard Tad telling Mike he might go to Alberta and have better luck there. I hope he's kidding again.

After supper we took down the Christmas tree to make space for our guests on New Year's. Now the house looks so empty! I put a few of the cranes I'd made around the living room as decorations. They're symbols of good luck, so Mama approved.

Wednesday, December 31

Busy all morning washing mounds of rice, chopping vegetables, then cleaning all the dirty pots and pans. The house smelled like vinegar because of the *sushi!* After lunch I asked Mama if I could see a matinee and she gave me the afternoon off. And I didn't have to take Harry because he was too busy playing with his Meccano set and didn't want to come! Maggie, Sachi and I saw *Broadway Melody of 1940* with Fred Astaire and Eleanor Powell. They danced a fancy number to "Begin the Beguine" — what a great swing song.

Today's *New Canadian* had an article about that *Nisei* soldier from the Island going overseas. After supper Tad read us what Private Kato said. I was so impressed, I'm copying it here:

Canada is the country I owe everything to and it's the one I want to fight for. All we want is a chance to prove our loyalty. After all, the outside appearance of a man doesn't matter. It's what is inside that counts.

Tad said, "Amen to that!" and I do too.

1942

Thursday, January 1

Omedetō gozaimasu 1942. Happy New Year and goodbye 1941! We went to early mass, so I'm writing here this morning for a change, because everyone is too busy to notice I haven't anything to do!

New Year's is almost a bigger holiday than Christmas for us. I love the special plates, bowls and other things we use today that Mama brought with her from Japan. My favourites are the ceramic chopstick rests shaped like miniature vegetables such as carrots and eggplants. Today we'll eat all sorts of strange food — by Canadian standards — but I enjoy most of them. Harry loves the tiny dried fish, I like the sweet black beans and Tad and Mike are crazy for Mama's *ozōni*. Most of the dishes have symbolic meaning, or so Kay and Emma tell me, but I just eat them!

Mama's calling me, so I'd better go — there's still lots to do!

Later

The Nakagawas visited today and I was happy to see Gladys again. She and Emma met for the first time — they really are quite alike. Mrs. Nakagawa gave us some of her homemade strawberry jam. Mama says it's so much better than even the fancy Empress brand from the stores.

The Hiranos arrived and brought us some yummy *senbei*. The Yamadas came too — I was glad to see Sachi. People came and went all day, especially a lot of Papa's friends from his club, and older men like Mr. Murata from next door. Geechan enjoyed himself because he had lots of people to talk with in Japanese! Everyone admired his two beautiful *bonsai* on top of the piano.

Mama, Kay and Emma were busy bringing out food and washing dishes. I helped dry for a while. Even Mr. Franklin dropped in for a drink with Papa, but he didn't eat anything. He apologized for Mrs. Franklin not coming, but we knew she wouldn't. She never has, the entire time we've lived here. Danny would have, if he'd been around!

And every year Papa invites Mr. Cowan, but this year he actually came! He was wearing a suit and tie — it was funny seeing him out of the white coat he always wears in the drugstore. We were very honoured to have him visit our home.

Papa offered him some *sake,* which he said he liked. I'm not sure he enjoyed the various foods he tasted, but at least he was willing to try. Later he even joined Harry and me in a game of Snakes and Ladders in a corner of the living room. And before he left, he gave us each a Lowney's chocolate bar!

I'm feeling much more positive with the new year. I hope it'll be a good one for everybody.

Friday, January 2

Papa, Tad and Mike went back to work today. When Mike came home, he said things are so slow at the lumberyard he's not sure he'll be working much longer. But Papa and Tad are very busy at the drugstore. Mama's busy too, with people bringing clothes in to be altered or repaired. That's good, since she can't work at the newspaper anymore. Kay said her hours at Maikawa's will be cut back now that the holidays are over, but she'll have more time to help Mama with her sewing.

Saturday, January 3

The Vancouver papers say that "enemy aliens" in the United States — Japanese, German and Italian — must surrender their cameras and radios, and it may happen *here*. I hadn't heard that phrase before, so I looked it up. It means "a citizen of a country at war with the country in which he or she resides."

I shouldn't get anxious over what's happening in the States. It couldn't happen *here*. Most Japanese

Canadians were either born here like us or are naturalized like Mama and Papa.

When he got home tonight, Papa gave Harry and me a quarter each. I hope the gang is free to go to the movies tomorrow. It's our last chance before school starts on Monday! I'd like to see *North West Mounted Police* with Gary Cooper. He's sooooo handsome.

Monday, January 5

It's good to be back at school. Things feel more like it was before Pearl Harbor. Even B.F. ignored me today! Everyone talked about what we did over the holidays and a few people asked about my New Year's resolutions.

I've only made one and I haven't told anybody, but I'm writing it down here. It's to stop worrying for no reason! I'm just going to concentrate on doing well at school, enjoying my friends and being nice to my family!

Thursday, January 8

Blackout is back on again — ugh! Harry's got another cold. The weather has been drearier than ever this year. And horrid Billy has started up following me again and making faces. I'm doing my best to ignore him.

Monday, January 12

I found a nasty cartoon torn from a magazine in my desk this morning. It showed a Japanese man with slanty eyes, round glasses and buck teeth. It's so sickening I can't possibly show anyone.

Billy must have put it there, but why? I'm not the only Japanese person in my class — there's Ken Murakami and Tak Narita. But maybe Billy doesn't pick on boys in case they fight back. Maggie, Ellen or Sachi couldn't have prevented this.

I'm so discouraged again. When we were walking home from school this afternoon, Ellen said, "Jeepers, Mary, you look awfully glum again. Is Billy bothering you?"

I couldn't possibly show her that drawing! I don't even know for sure if it was Billy who put it in my desk.

Wednesday, January 14

Heavy fog today. And cold drizzle too, so the streets were slippery for walking and driving. Our first choir practice this year was cancelled. Tad was late getting home and said doing deliveries was tough today with all the traffic problems.

He mentioned that a volunteer group of *Nisei* men might form to work on public-works projects to show the Japanese community's goodwill. He's thinking of joining since he hasn't been able to enlist, but Mike feels there's something fishy about it.

Still haven't told anyone about that horrid cartoon. At least there haven't been any others.

Friday, January 16

Mama's first tea night since before Pearl Harbor. All the ladies were anxious tonight. Mrs. Shimura insisted that those rumours about our radios and cameras are true — the Mounties really are going to take them away from us. I don't believe it!

Tuesday, January 20

I haven't written here because I'm down in the dumps about the latest bad news.

Last Saturday, the papers said Ottawa has created a "protected" area, one hundred miles in from the B.C. coast. It was on the radio too. All enemy aliens must leave this area. Surely the government doesn't really think of us as enemy aliens? If Japanese Canadians must leave, will Italian and German Canadians have to leave too? I'm trying not to worry, but it's hard without knowing what this could mean.

We're all concerned about Geechan now. It's a good thing he lives here in Vancouver, and the orders don't apply to anyone over the age of forty-five. Geechan must be at least sixty!

Wednesday, January 28

MORE bad news.

The papers say that west-coast American cities want Japanese Americans to be moved away — they call them "Japs." The *hakujin* there believe these people belong to a "fifth column" secretly helping the enemy. *Hakujin* in B.C. must think the same way if people born in Japan have to leave the coast. Papa says that any unemployed *Nisei* men are also being ordered to leave the protected zone. I hope Mike doesn't lose his job!

It's been more than two weeks since I found that nasty cartoon. I can't possibly show *anyone.* I really don't know what to do.

Saturday, January 31

Harry and I missed the earthquake last night! It happened just before eleven while we were sound asleep. Tad and Mike had just gone to bed and felt a strange vibration, but never imagined it was an earthquake. Nothing was damaged, although one person's baking was spoiled. The phone lines were jammed with calls to the papers because so many people thought the Japanese were up to something!

Tuesday, February 3

In Mr. Bell's Social Studies class today, we learned about propaganda. He said that because Canada's at war we encounter a lot of it. It means "an organized program of beliefs used to promote a certain idea or ideas. It can be used for both good and bad purposes." I copied that down exactly from the board.

Mr. Bell showed us some advertisements for the Victory Bond drive as good propaganda. Then he asked us for examples of the bad.

Diary, I don't know what made me do it, but I put my hand up and gave him that cartoon. He was surprised and asked me where it came from. I told him I found it in my homeroom desk. Mr. Bell said it showed exactly how propaganda can be used to distort the truth, and began to pass the cartoon around the class. When it got to Billy Foster, he turned beet red. I hope he'll leave me alone now!

Monday, February 9

Maybe I should just stop reading the newspapers if I don't want any more bad news. Today the *New Canadian* says that Alderman Wilson is trying again to make city council limit trade licences for "enemy aliens," especially the Japanese.

At least Alderman Jones said the idea wasn't "worth the paper it was written on." But why do some of these politicians hate us so much? Things are bad enough for us right now.

Today Papa and Mama said that any Japanese men who aren't naturalized or born here in Canada are being rounded up from coastal areas up north and sent away to work in the Rockies. That's crazy! Mama says most are fishermen whose boats have already been taken away. What on earth will they do in the mountains? I hope and pray this doesn't mean Geechan will have to leave us.

Tuesday, February 10

Guide meeting tonight. Evenings are so dark and gloomy now, I didn't want to go, but I'm glad I did. The girls came to get me and it was good being with our friends in the company. No one there makes me and Sachi feel like we don't belong! By the time the meeting was over, I felt much better. All the way home, the four of us practised the semaphore signals we'd learned.

Friday, February 13

Friday the 13th — I hope we don't get more bad news.

Later

We did.

At tea night, Mama's friends couldn't stop talking about the latest announcement — all male enemy aliens between the ages of eighteen and forty-five must leave the protected zone by April first. They're being sent to road camps in the Rockies near places no one knows.

Mrs. Oda is worried because her husband isn't naturalized. If he's sent away, how can she look after their five children by herself? Mrs. Matsumoto's oldest son was born in Japan while she was there visiting family, so now she's afraid he won't be considered Canadian, even though both she and her husband are naturalized and all their other children were born here.

Even worse, some men are being sent to a prisoner-of-war camp in Ontario, with barbed-wire fences and guards with *guns*. The papers call these men troublemakers, but Papa says they were just protesting being taken away from their families!

I can't believe this is happening. Isn't Canada supposed to be a democratic country? And what's going to happen to Geechan?

Saturday, February 14

More bad news, even on Valentine's Day. The government has started rounding up Japanese men who are not naturalized or Canadian citizens, right here in Vancouver. Like the others from the coast and the Island, they will have to go to work camps in the Rockies. Papa worries more about Geechan every day.

The two of them have been talking in Japanese every night now for over a week and I'm not sure what they're saying. But their voices sounded serious. Surely the government won't send Geechan away? He's too old! The *hakujin* believe these men will actually help Japan invade Canada. That's ridiculous. Geechan wouldn't hurt a fly — he's a Buddhist! I wish he'd been naturalized like Mama and Papa, who became Canadians before any of us were even born. Maybe he wouldn't have these problems now!

Monday, February 16

The bad news continues. The morning papers announced the fall of Singapore to Japan. The British and Australians have surrendered completely. At school, I felt like all the non-Japanese students were staring at me and any other Japanese kids. No one said anything, but Billy Foster smirked at me. The teachers treated us normally, thank goodness.

I hate this war. I hate being singled out for something I have nothing to do with.

Tuesday, February 17

The papers keep talking about "the Japanese problem." People are writing letters, demanding that our entire community here in B.C. be sent to another province. Papa's been looking so worried every night when he gets home from work, and Mama looks the same all day. I'm afraid to ask them if this might really happen.

Thursday, February 19

Now the papers say that no province in Canada wants any "Japs" and B.C. is going to have to solve its own problem. What will happen to us if we have to leave Vancouver?

Sunday, February 22

The gang came over to play Parcheesi this afternoon. We ended up talking about If Day that was held in Winnipeg on Thursday and Friday to raise money for the Victory Loan campaign. It was in all the papers and on the radio, and showed what could happen if the Nazis really invaded Canada.

I think If Day was a good idea. Men posing as Nazis arrested the mayor, several aldermen, Manitoba's premier and the entire cabinet. They burned books about freedom and democracy in front of the main library, closed churches and arrested teachers to make sure only the "Nazi truth" would be taught. Signs announced Nazi supremacy and the new rules people had to follow. All religious, ethnic or Jewish organizations had to close and turn over their money and property to the invaders. The main Winnipeg paper printed a special section with only Nazi views. Pretty scary, even if it wasn't real.

Maggie and Ellen talked about how Vancouver could do something similar to show how horrible it is when people lose their freedom. Except

Sachi said that if we had an If Day here, instead of Nazis there'd be fake *Japanese* soldiers taking over and arresting everyone. Then white people would hate the Japanese Canadians even more than they already do. She's right!

Tuesday, February 24

Guide meeting tonight. It's so dark out that it felt later than it really was, so we sang campfire songs all the way there. We learned to tie some different knots and played some new games, but it was even darker when we went home.

A *Nisei* from Edmonton has joined the army now, so Tad's hopeful about enlisting again. He's given up the idea of joining the volunteer civilian corps of Japanese Canadians. Instead, he's going to the recruitment office on his way to work tomorrow. He's so stubborn.

Wednesday, February 25

Another dreary day. On the radio tonight, total evacuation of Japanese Canadians from coastal areas was announced.

Tad was poring over the *New Canadian*, which we rely on for news more than ever. The radio and Vancouver papers make for nasty listening or reading — they call us "Japs" more than I can ever remember. Suddenly Tad said, "Oh, for Pete's sake!" and left the room. I picked up the paper and saw this headline: *Nisei Must Be Ready to Accept Injustice.* That must have been what made Tad so angry.

I know how he feels. Why should we simply accept injustice? Aren't we Canadian citizens and British subjects?

I'm glad I've got this diary to write down all my thoughts. Sachiko understands how I feel, but I'm not sure Ellen or even Maggie realizes just how horrible this is for us.

Thursday, February 26

Terrible news today for our family and all Japanese Canadians. I don't have to imagine what If Day would be like here, it's happening to us now! We have to turn in all motor vehicles, radios and cameras to somebody or something called the Custodian. Poor Papa's going to lose his car. And without our radio, how will we keep up to date? I can't possibly give up my camera! It's so small, I'm sure I can hide it somewhere. But if I keep it, will I get into trouble or cause problems for Mama and Papa?

The worst thing is that now we have a dusk to dawn curfew. How can Sachi and I get to Guide meetings? Mama can't have tea night anymore and her customers won't be able to drop off or pick up their mending in the evenings. Papa and Tad will have to go to work later and leave sooner, and so will Mike and Kay. We can't visit friends, go to the movies or do anything at night! This is SO unfair.

Friday, February 27

Yesterday the *News-Herald* had a special front page for the Victory Loan Campaign. It wasn't as dramatic as Winnipeg's If Day, but the headline was "STRENG VERBOTEN," which means strictly forbidden in German. Underneath were the rules to be followed if the Nazis took over.

But today's *New Canadian* did a clever thing. They made "STRENG VERBOTEN" a headline and listed two of those same rules for the Jews in Germany — curfew and turning in vehicles. Then right below, they reprinted articles from yesterday's *Province.* I've pasted them here:

Drastic Restriction   Ottawa Sets Up Curfew Law For All Coast Japs/All Ordered to Be In Homes By Sunset/AT ONCE/OTTAWA, Feb. 26 — (CP) — Japanese living within British Columbia coastal areas must remain in their homes between sunset and sunrise under a curfew order approved by the Dominion Government.

Strictly Forbidden OTTAWA, Feb. 27 — (CP) — Persons of Japanese race living in the protected area of British Columbia are forbidden possession or use of "any motor vehicle, camera, radio transmitter, radio receiving set, firearm, ammunition or explosive" under an amendment to the defence of Canada regulations, made known today.

What a daring way to show how horrible these new orders are for us! Tad was surprised the *New Canadian* was allowed to do this. Mike thought it was because it appeared on the second page!

Monday, March 2

The police caught twelve Japanese Canadians breaking curfew, including two milkmen out on their rounds before sunrise. They were all let go with warnings, but it's scared everyone. We don't dare go *anywhere* after dark.

The *New Canadian* reports that all our evening sports tournaments are cancelled — basketball, table tennis and bowling! Curfew has "rubbed out" sports in the community. But how can whoever wrote that go on to say: *We can take it. Crying over matters will not help . . . for what's to be done will have to be done.*

I simply can't believe people aren't more angry or upset!

Japanese men who aren't naturalized really *are* being sent away to road camps in the Rockies. Two farmers from Langley left last week, leaving behind their wives and children. Everyone's dismayed because families are being torn apart. I asked Papa what will happen to Geechan and he said he doesn't know.

Tuesday, March 3

Maggie and Ellen went to Guides tonight without me and Sachi, but not because of curfew. Today is Girls' Day — *Hina Matsuri*. I love it when Mama brings out our set of special dolls from Japan and puts them on display. Usually she unpacks them before the end of February, but this year she didn't get them out until last night. The dolls have been in Mama's family a long time. They once belonged to Aunt Eiko as oldest sister, but she never married and Aunt Aki only has boys, so Aunt Eiko gave them to Mama when Kay was born.

After Emma and I got home from school, we helped Mama arrange the dolls on the shelves of a stand covered in red cloth. The figures are dressed as the Emperor, Empress, musicians and other people of the court. There are miniature lanterns, furniture and trees. I love the dolls' beautiful costumes, but Mama kept sighing as we put the display together. Something is bothering her when she does that. She looked so serious I was afraid to ask what was wrong.

Papa left work early and went to Powell Street before dusk. He brought back some pink *sakura mochi,* a Girls' Day treat. He was lucky to find any because most shops were closing up because of curfew. We ate them with green tea after supper but we didn't feel festive. It didn't help when Papa said he saw big notices up on Powell Street ordering *all* people of the Japanese race to leave the protected zone. It doesn't matter if you are naturalized or born in Canada. I can't believe it.

Vancouver General Hospital dismissed three *Nisei* nurses in training. One of them is the sister of Emma's friend Yoshiko. Emma was really distressed at the news because she hopes to be a nurse herself one day. I'm really worried and scared about what might happen next.

Wednesday, March 4

This morning after breakfast Mama wrapped the *Hina* dolls in extra newspaper and put the box into a bigger wooden crate. She also packed away the box of Boys' Day banners that we usually bring out on May 5. Mama stuffed some straw around the boxes and asked Mike to nail the crate shut. Then she wrapped it up tightly with sturdy string. When I asked what she was doing, she said she was making sure the dolls and banners will be kept somewhere extra safe. Sachi told me her family just put their dolls back in their attic like they always do.

Thursday, March 5

Mama must have known what might happen. The *New Canadian* confirmed that everyone must now turn over our property and belongings to the Custodian of Enemy Alien Property as a "protective measure." Now we are *all* enemy aliens, not just those born in Japan! Why do our property and belongings even need protection? Tad said Mama labelled the crate of Girls' and Boys' Day things with Aunt Aki's address in Montreal. Then she asked him to take it to the CPR station and have it shipped. I suppose we'll get the crate back sometime. But what about our other belongings? We can't possibly ship everything we own to Aunt Aki!

Papa was also very angry today when he got home from work. He explained there's now something called the B.C. Security Commission taking charge of the Japanese Canadian community. One of the men this commission hired to help them is a Mr. Morii. Papa said it was an unfortunate choice and Geechan shook his head in agreement. Mama called it disgraceful. When I asked why, Tad replied angrily, "Because he's a bully and an extortionist!"

I asked what that last word meant. Papa said it's someone who forces others to pay money for protection. I still didn't understand, so Tad said that this Mr. Morii runs a Powell Street gambling house as well as a *jūdō* club. If somebody refuses to pay for protection, he sends men from the club to beat them up. Apparently this really happened to certain shopkeepers. But no one will talk about it or tell the police in case they're beaten again!

No wonder Papa and Mama are upset about Mr. Morii working for the Security Commission. I thought being picked on by Billy was bad, but I'm disgusted that someone from our own community could be so wicked.

Friday, March 6

For days now, the papers have carried shocking stories about what the Japanese have been doing in Hong Kong and elsewhere. I can't even bear to think of those things, let alone write about them here. Papa doesn't want me reading these accounts. They are so sickening, he may be right. Maybe they're one reason why the *hakujin* hate us so much.

At supper tonight, Kay told us she was coming home on the streetcar when a *hakujin* lady sitting beside her asked her if she was Chinese or Japanese. Kay replied she was Japanese and the lady said, "It's terrible what you people are doing in this war." Then she got up and moved to another seat!

"You people"? Why can't these *hakujin* understand that we have nothing to do with those Japanese soldiers? I hate what they've done as much as anyone.

Monday, March 9

I dread every time the papers arrive. I didn't think things could get much worse but I was wrong. To start it was just men born in Japan and not naturalized who were sent to road camps. The first group left a few weeks ago. But now even Canadian-born men as well as naturalized *Issei* have to leave the coast. I'm so worried about my family. We don't know when this could happen, but there's nothing they or we can do about it. I can't stand feeling so helpless! Papa's been naturalized for twenty-five years and Tad and Mike were *born* here. Why won't the government recognize our loyalty to Canada?

And as if I don't have enough to worry about, Billy has started following me again. To avoid him, I've been leaving homeroom quickly and rushing to my next class. He tried saying something to me in the hallway this morning but I ran away — luckily the monitors didn't see me!

Tad saw big signs on the North Shore highway today that said *Japs Keep Out!* I can't understand what's happening anymore.

I hope Sachi and I can get to Guides tomorrow. We'll be devastated if we can't!

Tuesday, March 10

We did it! Sachi and I got around curfew and stayed at Guides for the whole meeting!

Sachi had supper with us tonight. Then Maggie and Ellen came here and the four of us walked quickly to the church. Sachi and I told our leaders that we might have to leave early because of curfew. They were surprised and said they'd accompany us home if necessary. But it began to rain about an hour into the meeting. Maggie had brought along her father's big black umbrella and she had a brilliant idea. We four would all huddle underneath the umbrella and hope no policeman would notice that two of us were Japanese. All for one and one for all! Miss McLeod asked me to phone her when we got home so she'd know we arrived safely. Maggie's idea worked!

The only thing that wasn't nice was that when I tried to call Miss McLeod, the people who share our party line were on the phone already. Somebody said, "Why don't you get your own line, you stupid Jap!" I was so shocked, I put the receiver down and waited five minutes before calling Miss McLeod.

Wednesday, March 11

Managed to avoid Billy today. Harry listened to his last *Lone Ranger* program tonight. Our radio has to go by week's end.

Mama said that the Hiranos had their home searched by Mounties. They had already turned in their camera and radio and said how unpleasant it was having someone going through their personal belongings. I can't imagine Mounties coming here and looking through our home. I've hidden my camera in a safe place for now — sure hope no one finds it. I don't want to get myself or anyone in my family into trouble. We have enough to worry about already!

People have started turning in their cars to the

impounding centre at the Hastings Park racetrack. Nobody wanted to sell to the used-car dealers trying to buy from them. Instead, they did as asked by our government and gave up their cars or trucks to the Custodian of Enemy Property. The RCMP barracks at 33rd and Heather was busy too, with people turning in cameras and radios. It all feels so unreal.

Thursday, March 12

When I got home from school, Mama said a Mountie came today and told Geechan he has to go to a road camp in the Rockies and must be at the train station on Monday.

At supper tonight, everyone was miserable except Geechan. He kept saying, *"Shikata-ga-nai"* — it cannot be helped. Geechan is much older than the forty-five-year age limit for sending the *Issei* away. I think it's disgraceful taking an old man away from his family to do hard labour in some desolate place in the Rockies! Maybe he should have gone back to Japan before Pearl Harbor. He still has family back in Nagasaki. He might have had a comfortable life there instead of being treated like a criminal in Canada!!

Friday, March 13

No one came for tea tonight. Everyone is afraid. A man was arrested for breaking curfew the other day and sentenced to six months in jail! Mama says

I'd better be extra careful on Guide nights or I can't go anymore.

When Mike came home he said that tomorrow is his last day at the lumberyard. Mr. Yamamoto has no trucks to pick up or deliver supplies, so there's little work. I hope that Mike won't be sent away next!

And Aunt Eiko has lost her bookkeeping job for that company on Powell Street that imports goods from Japan. Japanese ships haven't been able to enter Canada ever since we declared war against Japan after Pearl Harbor. Aunt Eiko doesn't know what she'll do for money now.

Geechan's been praying more in front of his little shrine lately. I should be saying prayers for all of us, too.

Saturday, March 14

Today Papa asked Kay to see if Mrs. Franklin would like our radio. Kay came back from next door furious. Mrs. Franklin didn't want the radio because she was afraid of receiving enemy messages on it. How ridiculous! We ended up giving it to Kay's friend Audrey Young over on Triumph Street. Mr. Young told Papa if he ever wanted it back, just to let him know.

Even though the news on the radio upsets me, how can we keep informed without it? Thank goodness the *New Canadian* can still publish. Harry is really disappointed that he can't listen to *The Lone Ranger* anymore. And we'll all miss the big-band shows. At least Tad and Mike brought their portable gramophone upstairs so we can still hear some music. Life is becoming very dull but at the same time full of worry.

Sunday, March 15

Geechan leaves us tomorrow. Everyone's been really glum — even Harry was quiet at our farewell supper tonight. Mama cooked Geechan's favourite dishes but nobody ate much. She made sure Geechan packed lots of warm clothes and a mackinaw jacket because it's going to be very cold in the mountains. I can't stand the thought of him going away!

Monday, March 16

Rags knew something was wrong this morning. He followed Geechan everywhere until it was time for him to go. Papa thought it would be too sad if we all went to the train station, so only he and Tad did. The rest of us said our goodbyes here. I tried really hard not to cry. Geechan looked so stern in his coat and hat. I handed him a box of Maple Buds I'd been saving and he finally smiled.

The house feels so empty without him. He even took his little shrine, but asked Papa to look after his *bonsai*. I've been feeling blue ever since we learned Geechan was leaving, and now he's really gone. Mama said Kay and Emma can move into his old room. I'll finally have my own bedroom, but I hate how this happened.

Tuesday, March 17

I managed to avoid Billy today because we had another air-raid drill at school. I took in our empty tin cans this morning for the scrap metal drive. We still have drives for Victory Stamps and a new one to raise money to send milk to British children. Some girls are knitting afghans for the Red Cross.

But, diary, here's the truth. My heart isn't into the war effort now that Geechan's gone and Mike could be sent away any time too, never mind Tad and Papa! I don't know how Sachi stays so optimistic. She's making afghan squares, just to have something to do in the evenings during curfew and it helps towards her Knitter badge. I'd rather be reading but I have to find another good book.

In English Lit. today, Miss Wright read "The Song My Paddle Sings," a poem by a Canadian writer named Pauline Johnson. It made a nice change from the usual British stuff! Miss W. suggested we might enjoy one of Miss Johnson's collections of poetry or even her book of short stories called *Legends of Vancouver*.

At Guides tonight, I asked Miss Alston if she'd

heard of Pauline Johnson and she had! Next week she'll bring in more information and thanked me for a good discussion topic.

Sachi and I got home safely, using Maggie's umbrella trick again. Thank goodness Vancouver is drizzly so often.

Wednesday, March 18

I'm still missing Geechan badly.

Mike's been pounding the pavement this week, looking for a job. So far, no luck. At this rate, he'll need new shoes.

Thursday, March 19

I signed out *Legends of Vancouver* from the school library and am really enjoying it. The tales are all about places I know. Miss Johnson met a Squamish chief who told her many of his people's traditional stories. She found them so interesting that she wrote them down and these are the legends in the book.

Reading *Legends* helps to pass these dreary evenings when we can't go out on account of curfew. My big brothers and sisters say they're bored to tears stuck inside the house. They need to find some good books too!

Saturday, March 21

Tad and Mike got into serious trouble last night. Tad told Papa they were meeting some friends on

Powell Street after work and to let Mama know the two of them wouldn't be home for supper. Papa thought they'd be back before dark but they weren't. By 9 p.m., Mama and Papa were anxious. Harry asked if Tad and Mike had been arrested, so Kay put him to bed! Mama was so distracted, I stayed up longer than usual. But it was getting later and later with no sign of my brothers. Papa began telephoning the homes of all their friends, but nobody knew where they were. Mama was so worried she couldn't even sew. I finally went to bed but I was worried too.

This morning Emma explained what happened. Tad's friend Fred Yu told him that these days some Chinese people are wearing special buttons that say *I am Chinese,* so they won't be mistaken for Japanese! Most *hakujin* can't tell the difference. Tad asked Fred to get some of those buttons for him and Mike, so they could go out in the evenings again!

Tad and Mike arranged to meet Fred at an ice cream parlour in Fairview before dusk. Fred brought his sister and two of her friends. The six of them had something to eat, saw a movie and then went bowling! My brothers came home on the streetcar and were still wearing the buttons when they walked in the front door after midnight.

Mama was livid and told them they were thoughtless and impertinent! Papa was just relieved they were safe. Tad and Mike got a very long lecture from Mama in Japanese before they could go to bed. She took away their buttons. And she made them promise they'd NEVER do something like that again!

Monday, March 23

When I got home from school today, Harry was sulking and wouldn't say what was wrong, but Emma eventually got him to tell. Some boy called him a dirty Jap at recess and told Harry to go home to Japan. Harry said he was *born* in Canada and his home was right here on Oxford Street. The two of them started fighting but Harry's teacher turned up and asked the other boy to mind his own business.

After he told his story, Harry burst into tears! Rags knew Harry was upset — he tried to lick Harry's face. Emma gave Harry a cookie and he finally stopped wailing. Kids can be so mean to each other. As if I don't I know already!

Tuesday, March 24

The weather is still cold and miserable. I hope Geechan is okay wherever he is. Vancouver has a fuel shortage but we haven't run out of coal yet. Papa has been lighting fires in the living-room fireplace, so it's a little cheerier at night. Made it to Guides and back safely again!

Tonight Miss Alston talked about Pauline Johnson, who was part Mohawk. She became famous reciting her poems in England, the U.S.

and Canada, including British Columbia. She loved canoeing, camping and nature — she'd have made a great Guide leader! — and she's buried right here in Stanley Park. I'd like to see the plaque dedicated to her next time we go there.

I told everyone how interesting Miss Johnson's stories are and how they describe places we'd all recognize, like the Lions. The Squamish legend calls them the Two Sisters!

Wednesday, March 25

I feel terrible again. Mike got orders to go to road camp today. Like Geechan, he's being sent somewhere near Alberta and must leave next week. Mike said he's lucky, because his friend Ron only had seven hours to get ready! Tad told Mike he should be glad he wasn't going to the Hastings Park Clearing Pool first, so I asked Mike why. He said all the Japanese moved from their homes on the coast or the Island must go to the park first. The Exhibition grounds are being converted so people can live there until they're sent somewhere else. It sounds unbelievable!

Mike hasn't said anything but I can tell he's upset about having to leave us. He told Papa and Mama he'll wire them as much of his wages as he can. He was making fifty cents an hour working at the lumberyard, but the Security Commission only pays twenty-five cents and deducts the cost of his accommodation and food! The only thing Mike asked was whether he could take the gramophone and some of his favourite records with him. Since he and Tad bought them with their own money, everyone agreed. They're unusual items for road camp, but Mike loves the big bands. Tad said if he ends up in the army, he couldn't use them anyway, so Mike may as well!

Saturday, March 28

We don't have a car anymore. Mr. Cowan bought it from Papa for a good price, saying it seemed like it belonged to Cowan's Pharmacy already, with all the trips Tad had made for the store. And Tad couldn't drive it anyway. The latest order requires any Japanese Canadian to have a permit from the RCMP to travel "for any purpose whatsoever."

We're lucky we could sell our car. So many of Papa's friends just turned theirs in at Hastings Park for a receipt and a promise they'll be reimbursed later. It must be terrible for people who need cars or trucks for their businesses, like Mr. Nakagawa. I asked Mama what would happen now to the Nakagawas' farm without any trucks to deliver the berries in the summer. She didn't know.

At supper Mama described something terrible she learned from Mrs. Shimura. When curfew first began, an elderly man was living alone in a Powell

Street rooming house. He was very ill and probably dying, so his daughter asked for a permit to see him. She was turned down, as was the man's Japanese doctor. The poor man died all alone! And all because of curfew. So far only a few Japanese doctors and dentists have been given permits to see patients after dark.

I want to cry when I hear things like this are happening here in my own city and my own country.

Sunday, March 29

Yesterday's *New Canadian* had a huge notice "TO ALL MALES OF JAPANESE RACIAL ORIGIN." All men eighteen or over in the Vancouver area must report to the RCMP. Since Mike is already leaving, that means Tad and Papa. If they don't, they have to pay a $500 fine and go to jail for a year!

The *New Canadian* has moved into the offices of Mama's newspaper. They need the Japanese typefaces to print articles in Japanese. The government finally realized that some people can *only* read Japanese. The paper is being censored now. I guess the government finally found someone who can read Japanese!

Tuesday, March 31

I feel wretched. We said goodbye to Mike early this morning. Papa looked glum and Mama was trying hard not to cry, so I tried, too, but it didn't work. Kay and Emma did a better job but Harry was bawling. It was grey and drizzly out, just like our feelings. Tad and Papa took the streetcar to the train station with Mike. They helped carry his luggage — one suitcase of clothes and a box with the carefully packed gramophone and records. Mike had to show the Mounties at the station that the record player wasn't a radio! Papa and Tad couldn't even wait for Mike's train to leave because they both had to report to the RCMP barracks before going to work.

I was just getting used to Geechan not being with us and now Mike's gone too. We were all very dejected at supper tonight, especially Papa and Mama. I went to my bedroom after eating and said I was going to read, but instead I cried some more.

I said a prayer for Mike's safety and Geechan's, too. I also prayed that Tad and Papa won't be leaving next.

Wednesday, April 1

April Fool's Day. We're all missing Mike and feeling so rotten, no one even played any tricks this morning.

Thursday, April 2

Tad's still working in Cowan's stockroom. He does the smaller deliveries on a bicycle Mr. Cowan brought in. Mr. Cowan hasn't found a driver for the car yet.

Mama went to Powell Street to buy fresh salmon for tomorrow's Good Friday supper. She says she sees a lot more *nihonjin* on the streetcars these days because so many have lost their cars. But with gasoline rationing starting this month, she might see more *hakujin* too.

Good Friday, April 3

No school for me and no work for Papa today. We all went to church this morning. I always find Good Friday so depressing, and I was already feeling dismal. At least it's a long weekend.

Easter Sunday, April 5

The Easter bunny brought Harry a chocolate rabbit from Purdy's. I received something more practical, pairs of socks in different colours. But I also got a box of Maple Buds, which reminded me of Geechan and made me sad. We haven't heard from him yet, even though he's been gone almost three weeks. But Papa says any letters from men at road camp must go to Ottawa first to be read by censors before we get them.

Early mass was crowded this morning. Today is the vernal equinox, when there is as much daylight as darkness. It means the days are getting longer and it's brighter earlier and later, so curfew is easier to bear.

We had ham for Easter dinner. Aunt Eiko came over around noon and announced that she has a new job. She's doing secretarial work for the Security Commission, of all things! They like that she speaks English as well as Japanese and has office experience. She'll be helping out at Hastings Park. Mr. and Mrs. Hirano came for dinner too. I know we all had to squeeze around the dining-room table before, but I really missed Mike and Geechan today.

Thursday, April 9

Kay's job ends this Saturday. Business has slowed down at Maikawa's after Easter. It's been slowing down in the Powell Street shops anyway with all the uncertainty. People are unwilling to spend money in case they need it later. At least Kay won't be sent away somewhere because she's out of work!

Tuesday, April 14

Sachi and I got to Guides tonight without Maggie's father's umbrella. It's light enough now that we can get home before dark. Hurray!

The cherry and apple trees in our backyard are blossoming. So are most of the flowering trees in the city. They look so pretty, but they remind me of Geechan. He liked to sit outside this time of year and look at the flowers. I'd like to write to him but we don't know where he is yet. And besides, he can't read much English and I can't read or write Japanese. I hope he's well, and Mike too!

Wednesday, April 15

At supper tonight Harry mentioned a new board game the kids at Hastings Elementary are playing. It's his birthday soon, so Kay asked him to describe it. He said it's called Yellow Peril! We stared at him in disbelief as he went on to explain how a few brave defenders can fight a great number of enemies.

Everyone was dead silent until Emma finally told Harry he would NOT be receiving that particular game. Then she explained that "yellow peril" is what *hakujin* call the Japanese who might invade North America. It's a phrase being used to convince people that *all* Japanese are evil. Harry said he was sorry, but Mama told him this showed why he shouldn't want what everyone else wants. Wartime propaganda again!

Still no letter from Geechan. He's been gone a month now.

Friday, April 17

When I got home from school today, Mama and my sisters were all talking at once. It took a while to find out why they were so upset. Aunt Eiko had told Mama that their old friends the Haradas are here in Vancouver, so Mama went to see them this morning. The Haradas used to live in Prince Rupert, but the family was forced to move last month. Since then they've been living at Hastings Park. After what Mama described, no wonder Tad thought Mike was lucky he didn't have to go there!

The families evacuated from the coast really are living in the Exhibition buildings. There are barbed-wire fences around the park and guards check everyone coming in and going out. What a dreadful place for Aunt Eiko to work!

Mrs. Harada and her three children are sleeping in a cattle stall in the livestock building! It smells disgusting and they have to share one straw mattress. Hundreds of mothers and children are crammed together — the only privacy they have are some sheets and blankets the women have hung up.

The toilet facilities are wretched. There's just an open trough without seats or walls and there are only ten showers for ALL THOSE PEOPLE! The Haradas can't even be together as a family. The children and Mrs. Harada are all in one building, but Mr. Harada is in another and they aren't allowed to visit each other! They've been there almost a month and Mama said they looked tired and unwell.

The family is having a hard time eating the food provided because they only ate Japanese food at home. Mama saw people waiting in a long line for lunch — a slice of bologna and a piece of dry bread, served on a tin plate. There were no fruits or vegetables and only black tea or coffee.

Mr. Harada was angry at being separated from his family and tried to protest. Maybe because of that, he's going to be sent away tomorrow! And Mrs. Harada and the children must go somewhere else, to one of the places where the Japanese are now being ordered to go. Mama calls them "ghost towns." I wondered why they're called that, but everyone was so worked up, I couldn't ask.

So now Mama is putting together a package of Japanese food and fresh fruit for the Haradas. Kay and Emma are going with her to deliver everything tomorrow. Aunt Eiko got them special passes to get in.

The last thing to infuriate Mama is that there's no school at Hastings Park even though the two oldest Harada kids should be going. Mama and Papa have always stressed the importance of a good education to us. We need it to succeed in the future and get good jobs.

I've never seen Mama so cross about anything before! At times, I wasn't sure I really understood what Mama was saying. She was so distressed, she could only speak rapidly in Japanese. But my sisters say it's all true. Kay calls the situation barbaric and Emma is going to write to the Security Commission and anyone else she can think of, to complain.

I should feel lucky that our family hasn't had to leave our home, and that we eat well and I'm still in school, but I don't. I don't feel very good about *anything* right now.

Saturday, April 18

Mama and my sisters went to Hastings Park this morning. When they came back, Harry asked if they went on any rides. Kay rolled her eyes but Emma explained that Hastings Park isn't an amusement park anymore, it's where Japanese people are being kept until they are sent away. Harry wanted to know if they've been bad and are being punished, like at school. Emma said that's the big difference — Japanese Canadians have done absolutely nothing to deserve this treatment.

Emma also explained what the "ghost towns" are. They're places in the interior that used to be prosperous mining centres but have fallen on hard times. The towns agreed that the evacuated Japanese could live there to help their economy. The Commission isn't calling them ghost towns, though. They're "relocation centres."

Sunday, April 19

Papa's planting a garden and asked Harry and me to help him look after it. It will be smaller than the one Geechan put in, but Papa says fresh vegetables are best and cheaper than what we can buy in the shops.

Tuesday, April 21

Mama took more food to Hastings Park today for the Haradas. Still no word on where the family will be sent. Mama said it is so sad to see people in such shameful living conditions. She told us maybe it was sacrilegious, but she wished Father Benedict would pray during mass for the Japanese here in B.C., because right now they need God's help almost as much as our soldiers do.

Monday, April 27

I am a wreck. I'm losing my family one by one.

Tad took me aside after supper tonight. He knew how upset I was when Geechan left and then Mike, so he waited until the last possible moment to say he's leaving us too! But he's not going because he has to. He *volunteered* to go east with the other *Nisei* ordered to a work camp in northern Ontario. He made up his mind a while ago and doesn't want me to worry about him.

He's heard that people in Ontario aren't against us the way they are here in B.C. He told his plans to Mr. Cowan and Mama and Papa after Easter. Even Kay and Emma knew and kept it secret! I was the last to know besides Harry, who found out while I was busy giving Rags a bath. Tad didn't say so, but I think he'll try to enlist out there. I'm so upset I can't write another thing.

Tuesday, April 28

I'm feeling just awful and not because I missed Guides. Tad left for Ontario tonight. He's headed somewhere called Schreiber. But because he volunteered, he was free to get to the train station on his own. That's a blessing, given what we saw! The men who came from Hastings Park directly to the train station arrived in old buses guarded by Mounties with their guns out! I recognized the Nakagawas' two youngest sons but the oldest wasn't with them.

Everyone hugged Tad goodbye, even Papa, but when it was my turn I stared at the ground. Tad asked me not to worry, and even though I tried not to, I began to cry. Tad squeezed me and whispered to be brave for the rest of the family and to look after Harry. I promised I'd do my best!

The old train the *Nisei* boarded wasn't much better than the old buses. Everyone on the platform was madly waving and calling goodbye or *sayonara*. The train finally pulled away and Harry and I kept waving until it was a speck in the distance. Then Emma said we'd better hurry home because of curfew. The sight of those Mounties with guns made me rush back to the streetcar stop!

At home, I felt so rotten I went to my room and got out this diary to see if writing things down would help. It hasn't.

Wednesday, April 29

A letter from Mike arrived today! He sent it April 3rd, from somewhere inland, near Alberta, but the name of the place was blacked out! We have to write him care of the post office in Revelstoke, the closest town.

Mike says he's fine but camp conditions are crude. At first the men lived in tents, but now they're building cabins to keep out the cold. Those who arrived before Mike had to deal with tons of snow, lousy food, no water and no latrines. It's better now but "no picnic," as Mike writes. Many of the men are older and miss their families terribly. One of them is Mr. Nakagawa, who's really worried about his family and farm. Mike misses us all too. I bet he isn't using the gramophone much.

I hope Geechan is better off, wherever he is. We still haven't heard from him, and he left two weeks before Mike. I hope and pray everyone, including Tad and the Nakagawa boys, is okay.

Thursday, April 30

Mama phoned Gladys to say we saw Ben and Joseph leaving. That's when she learned that Gladys and her mother must leave their farm. They couldn't do the picking anyway without their workers, who have no way of getting there or are being sent away to road camps or the ghost towns. There are no trucks to deliver the berries either. The fruit is going to rot in the fields.

Gladys and her mother must be at Hastings Park on Monday. And Mas was arrested for refusing to go to road camp with his brothers! He argued with the Mountie ordering them to leave. Now he's in a prisoner-of-war camp called Angler in northern Ontario. His brothers went to Hastings Park without resisting because their mother was so upset about Mas. Gladys was relieved that we saw them at the train station.

It was Harry's birthday today and the Tillicum Club published his name in the *Province* this morning. We had a quiet celebration. Mama made a small cake and we sang "Happy Birthday" but things just don't feel right. I guess that's because they aren't.

Monday, May 4

Papa said the drugstore has a new stock boy. And Mr. Cowan finally found someone to drive the car for deliveries. Tad would be amused to know that the pharmacy needs two people to replace just one of him! I hope he's safe in Ontario by now.

Diary, I hope Papa won't be the next one in our family to leave us!

Tuesday, May 5

Sachi's father is being sent away! The family doesn't know where yet, but he must leave Friday. I feel terrible for her because I know how awful it is — Geechan and Mike had to leave and Tad's gone too, even though he left because he wanted to. Until now, Sachi's always kept a positive outlook through all the bad things that have happened since Pearl Harbor. But on the way to Guides tonight, she looked really dejected. Maggie and Ellen were sorry for Sachi, but neither of them can really understand what she's going through. And I'm so afraid for Papa now!

Wednesday, May 6

Mama went to visit Gladys and Mrs. Nakagawa at Hastings Park today. She said they are fortunate to have a corner stall with a little more privacy, but I'm so upset that these good people are being treated like this.

Friday, May 8

Sachi's father left for road camp today. For the first time I can remember, Sachi missed school. No wonder! I'm going to drop by her house tomorrow to try and cheer her up, though I don't have any idea how.

Saturday, May 9

Visited Sachi today and the whole Yamada family is so sad. Sachi and I went to her bedroom. She had a good cry and I did too. Sachi's father is the nicest man. I can't understand why anyone believes that he or Geechan or Mike is a threat to Canada's security. I tried everything I could think of to make Sachi feel better, and finally brought her my book of fairy tales. It might help to get her mind off her troubles, even for a little while. In the meantime, I wish I could find something to distract me from *my* worries.

Monday, May 11

Sachi was back at school today, but she wasn't herself and who can blame her.

We finally had a short letter from Geechan today! Papa had to tell us what he wrote. Geechan says it's been very cold and snowy where he is. He's very glad for the long johns Mama packed. He and the other men are living in tents and have to melt snow for fresh water. He says not to worry about him and he'll write again soon. The letter is six weeks old!

Geechan sounds okay, but I'm so upset that he's living in a tent. He doesn't deserve to be taken away from us and treated this way!

Tuesday, May 12

Sachi stayed home from Guides tonight. We missed her. At least she said she's enjoying the fairy tales.

Friday, May 15

I can hardly write this. Mr. Cowan told Papa he couldn't work in the drugstore anymore. He said he was very sorry, but it just wasn't possible to keep him on. He'd be happy to give Papa a good reference, and thought that maybe Papa could find a job helping at one of the pharmacies on Powell Street. Doesn't Mr. Cowan know most Powell Street businesses are closing down?

Papa gave us the news at suppertime and tried to joke about it by saying we won't be getting any more chocolate-bar treats. Harry said, "Aw, that stinks," but Emma gave him the look and he stopped talking. I think even Harry finally noticed how worried everyone is.

What will we do without Papa working? Kay thinks that Mr. Cowan probably believes Papa will be sent away like so many other Japanese in Vancouver, and has to be prepared for the worst. This certainly is the worst for us! Geechan's living in a tent in the mountains, Mike's money hasn't reached us yet and we don't even know what Tad is doing. And Mama's sewing earnings are slowly disappearing because most *hakujin* have stopped coming and her Japanese customers are being sent away! I'm so worried Papa will be sent away too, now that he doesn't have a job.

Tuesday, May 19

It was raining but Mama went back to Hastings Park today. She found out that Mrs. Harada and her children leave next week for a place called Kaslo in the interior. Aunt Eiko discovered that Mr. Harada had been sent to Lemprière road camp in the Rockies. She told Mama that the men there and in some other camps have begun protesting by refusing to work until they see their families. The Security Commission can't send them all to prisoner-of-war camps in Ontario, so they might get their wish. I hope so!

Mama saw Gladys and her mother again. Mrs. Nakagawa is very worried about her husband and her sons, especially Mas in Angler. Gladys said the men there have to wear uniforms with big red circles on the back to make better TARGETS for the guards.

I can barely believe it. How can this really be happening?

Friday, May 22

Empire Day today and also Sports Day at Templeton. There was no assembly but we sang "God

Save the King" and "O Canada" before the action got underway outdoors.

It's funny, but I forgot our troubles, if only for a while. And I won a medal! The rain let up long enough for all the events to take place. I competed in the fifty-yard dash, high jump, broad jump and softball throw. I was also on a relay team with Maggie, Sachi and Ellen. Our team placed first, and because I scored highest in all my events, I won my division. Kay teased me but she admired my medal along with everyone else.

Sunday, May 24

I'm thirteen today. The gang treated me to a Double Decker at the Crystal Dairy. Maggie's brother still works there and still calls me Button Beak. It was so nice of Sachi to come because I know she's really missing her father.

Later I helped Papa in the garden. It reminded me of Geechan and I started feeling blue again. But I mustn't cry on my birthday. Kay says it means I'll cry every day for the rest of the year. I certainly don't want that!

Tuesday, May 26

Aunt Eiko told Mama there's now a kindergarten at Hastings Park and classes are being organized for the older children. The government still won't organize a proper school, so the teachers are mostly volunteer *Nisei* high-school students. It's too late for the Haradas, though. They left today for Kaslo. And Gladys and Mrs. Nakagawa have gone to Greenwood, another internment camp in the interior near the town of Castlegar.

Thursday, June 4

Our first letter from Tad came today! He and his friends are clearing bush for a highway. Camp conditions at Schreiber are basic, but the local people are friendly. They were amazed that Tad and the others could speak such good English!! He thinks he won't stay in Schreiber very long though. The *Nisei* are being offered better work on farms in southern Ontario. Tad figures he'll make more money if he leaves. He'll let us know where he's going if he does.

He misses us and hopes Mr. Cowan is managing without him. He doesn't know yet that Papa isn't working at the drugstore anymore. Kay's written him but her letter must not have reached him.

No letters from Mike or Geechan. It's so hard not hearing anything from them.

Friday, June 5

Good news — Kay found a job! But the bad news is that she's moving out. Her friend Eileen was working as a companion to a rich lady who used to be an actress. But Eileen's family is leaving next week for one of the ghost towns. Eileen promised Mrs. Mitchell that she'd find someone to replace her, and she asked Kay. She starts Monday!

Kay's excited because Mrs. Mitchell lives in a big house on Wall Street, not that far from us. She's married to an army colonel who's away a great deal, so she's often alone. Kay's supposed to do light housekeeping and prepare meals. It's not the kind of glamorous job I'm sure Kay would prefer, but at least it's work. Her earnings will help us a lot now that Papa's lost his job.

Monday, June 8

Kay left early to start her new job. Mrs. Mitchell sent over a taxi for her! Kay took a suitcase of clothes and kissed us all goodbye. I gave her an *origami* crane I'd folded last night for good luck.

Rags must wonder why everyone is disappearing. He followed me around the house after I got back from school. I really miss Kay already. She likes teasing me but she's a good egg and would do anything for me. She'll still be able to come home and visit because she has a day off every two weeks. It seemed very lonely at supper tonight with only five of us.

Tuesday, June 9

No time to write in my diary. I have a Latin exam tomorrow, so the gang went to Guides without me tonight. I've got to review all the verb conjugations. Ugh!

Saturday, June 13

I wrote my last exams yesterday, thank goodness. This morning Maggie and I rode over to the Powell Street Grounds. The place felt so empty because the Asahi have been disbanded. Nearly all the players have been sent away. We sat on the bleachers and I felt sad remembering those wonderful games that I watched with my entire family here last year.

Tuesday, June 16

Guide night again. Sachi was more like her old self tonight. I've been so worried about Papa that when I got home I asked Mama why he hasn't been ordered to leave yet like Sachi's father. Mama thought that perhaps because three men in our family have already left, the authorities haven't sent Papa away too.

Sunday, June 21

Today is the summer solstice, the longest day of the year. It's such a relief to be out later without worrying about curfew! The gang and I played extra sets of tennis, and then took Rags for a long walk around the neighbourhood. The sky was so beautiful, it's hard to believe our country is at war.

Monday, June 22

Everyone at Templeton was talking about the Japanese submarine attack on the Point Estevan lighthouse late Saturday night! Now Harry's interested in submarines, but I'm worried about how the *hakujin* here will react after a real Japanese attack on Canada. I hope it won't mean more bad news for us.

Friday, June 26

Last day of school! I made Templeton's honour roll again too. And no more Billy!

But this summer will be a long one. I can't go berry picking or to Guide Camp either. Now that Papa isn't working and Tad and Mike are gone, we must be careful about spending money. Mama's grateful that Kay gives her most of her earnings from Mrs. Mitchell's. Emma's going back to the fruit-packing factory this summer and will give Mama her wages too. Mike and Tad have also sent us some money, but no more letters!

Wednesday, July 1

Dominion Day. Record high temperatures in Vancouver yesterday — it was 105°! It's still very hot today. The dairies had a run on ice cream and some places were emptied out.

This morning Maggie and I got up early and rode our bikes to the harbour off Commissioner Street and went for a swim. Ellen's away and Sachi didn't want to come. The water felt great! But we were hot and sticky when we got back and had to wash the salt off our skin.

I don't feel very patriotic today. I kept thinking of the poor people stuck in Hastings Park in this heat. I bet they don't feel patriotic either.

Thursday, July 2

Another letter from Tad! It took almost a month to reach us. He left Schreiber and is now in St. Thomas, Ontario, on a sugar-beet farm. He says you need the back of an elephant and the brains of a mouse to do the work! He was sorry that Papa lost his job but will send us as much money as he can.

Monday, July 6

Aunt Eiko says that married men in road camps will be reunited with their families, but only in the relocation centres in the B.C. interior. They can't go back home. At least Mr. Nakagawa can be with his wife and daughter, and the Haradas can be together! But Geechan and Mike have no other family here except us, and we're still in Vancouver. I want us to be together again but I don't want to leave here!

Friday, July 10

Rationing starts in a few weeks, so people have been saving up what they can. We're lucky to have the extra sugar Kay gets from Mrs. Mitchell.

Tuesday, July 14

The school at Hastings Park had to close. It's too hot to hold classes.

Wednesday, July 15

Awful news. Papa received a letter written in Japanese today from someone at Geechan's road camp. No wonder we haven't heard from Geechan — he's ill! He's been taken to a hospital but the man didn't know where. The letter is dated May 27th! Papa's been on the phone ever since he read it, trying to find out where Geechan is and what's wrong with him. Mama's called Aunt Eiko to see if she can help. I'm so worried and there's nothing I can do!

Saturday, July 18

No news about Geechan. I'm sick with worry but Papa looks terrible. I hate not knowing what's happening.

Tuesday, July 21

We're all so anxious. Papa's worn out. He's spent all week trying to track down Geechan. Aunt Eiko is trying to find out which hospital Geechan might have been taken to. Prince George is a large town in the interior but it's difficult to reach from the camp. She's going to phone there tomorrow.

Thursday, July 23

When Aunt Eiko called the Prince George hospital, they said there's no patient named Kobayashi. Now she thinks that Geechan may have been taken to the Kamloops hospital instead. She's going to try calling there next.

Friday, July 24

More bad news! Sachi's family has to leave Vancouver next week. Mrs. Yamada is in a tizzy trying to pack because of all the rules and regulations about what can be taken and how much. Adults are only allowed one hundred and fifty pounds of luggage apiece and each child seventy-five. How can the Yamadas possibly cut down their whole life's possessions to that small amount? When I visited Sachi's house this afternoon, Mrs. Yamada was sorting through a trunk full of old *kimonos*, trying to decide which ones to bring. The family is leaving their good things in the attic until they return.

Sachi doesn't know where they're going yet, so I won't be able to write her! She says once she gets there, she'll write me so I'll know.

And Aunt Eiko can't get through to the Kamloops hospital. We're all still terribly worried about Geechan. Papa is exhausted and Mama's not much better. I've said a prayer for Geechan every night since we found out he's been ill, and I'm saying one again tonight.

Sunday, July 26
The gang got together today before Sachi has to leave. She's been busy helping her mother but Mrs. Yamada said she could play some tennis with us this afternoon. So the four of us went to Pandora Park, just like always. We played doubles but none of us said this might be the last time. When we finished, we were going to shake hands, but Ellen said, "Jeepers, Sachi, come here," and gave her a big hug instead. Then Maggie and I hugged Sachi too. The Musketeers are being split up!

Monday, July 27
Even Harry is feeling gloomy today. The Nine O'Clock Gun in Stanley Park is going to be silenced to save gunpowder.

❧

Wednesday, July 29

Spent the last two days crying my eyes out. I can hardly write this. Geechan was never a patient in the Kamloops hospital, because he died on the way. He was living in a tent with the other men at the Tête Jaune camp and the snow suddenly melted, flooding everything. Geechan got really sick after that — maybe it was pneumonia. The camp supervisor sent Geechan to the hospital. That was when that man wrote to Papa. But Geechan never made it there. Another man wrote Papa telling him what happened, but then everyone went on strike to protest being separated from their families. The mail wasn't sent until the strike was over. And then it was delayed by censors!

I was furious when we found out about Geechan, but Papa is so devastated, I could only cry. No one ever said how much it hurts when someone you love is gone forever.

Thursday, July 30

Sachi and her family left today. I went to their house to say goodbye, even though I'm feeling wretched. Sachi cried too when I told her about Geechan. We hugged each other and promised to stay in touch, no matter what. Then Sachi said she was so glad I was her friend because I understood how hard it is to be Japanese AND Canadian at the same time.

At least the Yamadas are supposed to meet up

with Sachi's dad wherever they end up. I'll never see Geechan again.

Monday, August 3

Papa received a package on Friday. Geechan was cremated but his ashes had to be inspected by government officials before they were mailed to Papa. We took a streetcar to the harbour yesterday after church, and I felt so numb I couldn't even cry as we watched Papa scatter Geechan's ashes in the water. Mama, Harry and my sisters were weeping, but I just stood there until I saw a tear roll down Papa's cheek. I reached for his hand and he squeezed mine back. Then I started to cry too.

Wednesday, August 5

Finally got a short letter from Mike today. He's been somewhere called Sandon since June. He and some other *Nisei* are fixing up old buildings for the families being sent there. He says the place reminds him of an old wild west town.

Emma is going to write him about Geechan. Harry wants her to ask Mike if there are cowboys in Sandon.

Saturday, August 8

I couldn't sleep last night because of the heat. The crickets chirping outside made me remember the cricket cage Geechan made for me. I can't bear to use it again, so today I buried the sticks in the backyard.

Wednesday, August 12

Ellen's dad gave her some money for her birthday, so she treated me and Maggie to Revels. Ellen started to say our Musketeer slogan — "All for one and one for all" — but then she realized that Sachi's gone and she stopped right in the middle.

Monday, August 24

The heat wave just won't stop. Our vegetable garden is shrivelling up and Papa doesn't seem to care. Geechan would never have let that happen.

Rationing has finally arrived. We have to use coupons from our ration books to buy sugar, coffee and tea.

Thursday, August 27

Mama says the Hiranos have left for a ghost town called Slocan City. She's so sad to see them go.

A short letter from Sachi arrived today. It's just three weeks old, maybe because it's in English. It's such a relief to hear from her. She and her family are living in some place called Lemon Creek in the Slocan Valley. And Mr. Yamada *is* back with his family, thank goodness.

Sachi says they now live in a tent because the houses aren't ready yet! There's no running water so she has to fetch it from outdoor pipes shared by many families. It's hard work and the water's so cold her hands are numb after washing rice for supper. There's no electricity either! But she sounds cheerful again, maybe because her father's there. I'll write her and mail my letter tomorrow.

Monday, August 31

Feeling blue again and don't feel like writing here.

Wednesday, September 2

This has been the worst summer of my life. Can't wait until school starts.

Friday, September 4

It's so unfair — I can't go back to Templeton! The Marchetti boys and the Schmidt kids CAN, even though Canada's at war with Italy and Germany!

Emma won't get her senior matric at Britannia High. She's really upset because she needs the diploma to become a nurse. And Harry can't start Grade Three. No Japanese Canadian students can return to school this fall.

Maggie tried really hard to cheer me up but it didn't work. What can she say or do that will change anything? She's a good friend, but she has no idea what it's like to feel so helpless. The ONLY good thing about this is I won't have to worry about Billy Foster.

Tuesday, September 8

It was strange not being in school today. Maggie promised to tell me everything that's happening at Temp this year. I wonder if Sachi can go to school where she is, or whether they even have a school there. I was going to read to keep my mind off things, but I've read all the books in the house and I can't use the school library anymore.

Thursday, September 10

Maggie's a peach! Today she brought home a few books for me from the school library, so at least I'll have something new to read. I've just started *Lorna Doone*.

And she told that me she and Ellen didn't join the school choir this year. They said it won't be the same without me and Sachi. Maggie may even quit Guides because Sachi's gone and I can't go anymore because of curfew, but I told her not to stop because of me!

We had another letter from Tad. He may go to Toronto to find work when the sugar-beet harvest is over in St. Thomas.

Monday, September 21

I'm in a funk not going to school. Grass hockey has started without me! Today is the first day of fall. The days are getting shorter, so curfew will be harder and harder.

Oxford Street feels so different. The Muratas left last week, so their house is all shuttered up and abandoned looking. Mama doesn't go to Powell Street anymore, since most of the shops are closed. We have few visitors now and the house is so quiet without Tad and Mike and Kay around. Nearly all the Japanese families have moved away. I'm worried we'll be next, but at least Papa is still with us.

Tuesday, September 29

Tomorrow Aunt Eiko leaves Hastings Park and goes to Kaslo. Most Japanese have been sent out of the protected area, so the Commission told her she'll be more useful helping people in the interior. She came to say goodbye tonight but had to leave before it got dark. She gave us all hugs and asked me to look after Harry.

Another family member leaving! I'm so upset, but there's nothing I can do.

Thursday, October 1

I haven't had much to write because (1) I've been really busy, and (2) I've been feeling too awful these days. Mama keeps saying, "So many hard choices to make." And then she mutters, *"Shikata-ga-nai."*

That's what she said when we had to give Rags away. We're leaving Oxford Street and can't take him with us. He's gone to Maggie's family, so I know he'll be well taken care of. I cried and cried when Maggie came to get him. She cried too. But there's been no time to feel sorry for myself because I have to pack.

Just like Sachi's mother, Mama has been anxiously going through our things, deciding what to take and what to leave behind. We're only allowed so much per person but I'm bringing my little camera, no matter what. I'll hide it well so we won't get into trouble!

And what's almost as bad as losing Rags is that I can't take my bicycle. Papa says it's not a necessity! All that work picking berries for nothing. I was angry when Papa told me but I know it's not his fault. And losing a bicycle is not like losing a fishing boat or a business. *Shikata-ga-nai* — how I dislike that saying! I gave my bike to Maggie.

Sunday, October 4

Kay came by today to pack up the things she wants when we leave Vancouver. She's told Mrs. Mitchell she has to leave soon and will give as much notice as possible. Harry's started sniffling, so I hope it's not another cold.

Tuesday, October 6

I had a short visit with Rags at Maggie's house tonight. Mama let me go to Guides one last time to say goodbye to my friends. Rags was so glad to see me, he licked my face like he'd never stop. He looked very confused when I left him behind, his head cocked to one side and his ears up.

When Maggie, Ellen and I got to the church, I told Miss McLeod my family is leaving Vancouver. She asked if we were going to the one of the internment camps in the interior like Sachi. I said until the Mounties tell us where we're being sent, for now we're moving to rooms above my mother's old newspaper office at Cordova and Gore. Miss Alston said, "Oh, in Japantown." I'd never thought of the area around Powell Street as Japantown, but there really are a lot of Japanese businesses there. Or there used to be. When the meeting ended, both leaders shook my hand and wished me all the best. Afterwards, Maggie, Ellen and I rushed out so I could get home before dusk.

Wednesday, October 7

Today Mama and Papa gave our refrigerator and wringer washer to the Youngs. The cast iron stove is too heavy to move and is staying behind with the piano. Papa even gave Geechan's *bonsai* to Mr. Young, since we can't take those either.

Rags came home yesterday afternoon! Harry and I found him in our backyard. He was so glad to see us, he ran around in circles. I hugged him and patted him for a long time. But eventually we used some string as a leash and took him back to Maggie's. When Mrs. Svendson tied him up in their yard, he looked perplexed and he made the saddest noises when we left. I couldn't look back when Harry and I went home.

Although we must leave our home, Mama says the rooms over the newspaper office are better than going to Hastings Park.

Thursday, October 8

We left Oxford Street this morning. Kay was lucky she wasn't here for this. I've never felt this bad in my life. Mama and Papa put all the boxes with our really good stuff in the attic, just like the Yamadas. We're only taking the everyday things to use while we're gone. The furniture is covered with old sheets. We took most of our luggage and parcels down to the newspaper office by streetcar earlier, but Emma and I went back to the house for a last farewell.

It was the hardest thing I've ever had to do. We walked through the rooms and I kissed the wall in each one goodbye. I thanked the house for being such a good home to us. I even went out to the backyard and kissed Geechan's fruit trees. And I said a prayer that we won't be gone long. The house looked so lonely when we finally closed the door.

Friday, October 9

I hate not being at home. It's not like when I went berry picking or when I went to Guide Camp, because I knew I was going home again. I miss Geechan and Mike and Tad and Sachi and Maggie and Rags and

Saturday, October 10

I just couldn't write any more yesterday.

It's hard to believe we've left Oxford Street. But it isn't for forever. We'll go back home again, I'm sure. The Guide motto is "Be prepared," so I'll try to look forward and not back.

We're living above Mama's newspaper office. There are lots of rooms up here, so perhaps this building used to be a boarding house. An old man, Mr. Nakamura, is staying here too. He has an enormous St. Bernard that drools a lot — Mama and my sisters think it's disgusting. But I don't think that Mr. Nakamura can bring his dog with him to the ghost towns. It's hard enough taking it out for walks because of curfew. The dog makes me feel sad, though, because it reminds me of Rags.

Monday, October 12

Today is Thanksgiving. I wanted to write that there's not much to be thankful for these days, but I'm trying to be positive because of that part of the Guide promise — to smile even under difficulty!

We actually had a pretty good Thanksgiving meal tonight. Kay brought over almost an entire turkey and all the trimmings she'd cooked yesterday. Mrs. Mitchell barely touched a thing and insisted that Kay bring us the leftovers.

We missed Geechan, Tad and Mike, the Hiranos and Aunt Eiko, but Mama asked Mr. Nakamura to join us. He said it was his first-ever Thanksgiving dinner and it was *oishii* — at least for Canadian food!

Wednesday, October 14

Harry's ill. He's always been a bit sickly and now he has a fever. Mama's quite worried. Papa went to the Powell Street Drugstore to get some Wampole's Vitamin Tonic because he thinks it might help.

Thursday, October 15

Things are getting even worse. Papa has been "detained." That's the word Emma used when Mr. Nakamura asked where Papa had gone. Some official-looking men came here this afternoon and asked Papa a lot of questions. Emma said they were

Mounties. Then they took Papa away in a car. Emma asked if he was being arrested and they said no, but he "was needed to help in their inquiries" — whatever that means. Emma phoned Kay and explained what happened.

I'm SO worried now, what with Harry being sick *and* Papa gone. I hope everything will be all right. I know crying won't help, but it's really hard not to. Emma can tell I'm anxious — she gave me a big hug tonight.

Friday, October 16

Dr. Kuwabara came to see Harry last night and sent him to St. Paul's Hospital. Mama is with him. I'm more worried than ever, especially because we don't know what's happened to Papa or where he is. I hope that he hasn't been sent to a road camp. Mr. Nakamura has gone now too. We don't know where he went either or what happened to his dog!

And to make things worse, today a Mountie brought papers for my sisters and me. We must leave Vancouver next week but we don't yet know where we're being sent. Kay gave Mrs. Mitchell notice and is joining us tomorrow — she says she needs to be here since both Mama and Papa are not!

I am really frightened and anxious. Tonight I'm praying for each and every one of my family. I hope God is listening.

Sunday, October 18

My sisters and I went to mass this morning at the Catholic mission down the street on Cordova. There were few people because most Japanese have left Vancouver now. I prayed hard for Harry to get better and for Papa to come back to us soon. And I prayed that our family will be reunited, no matter where we end up in the coming weeks.

The nuns at the mission were very kind. They said they've been writing the government since the spring to protest the treatment of Japanese Canadians, but it's made no difference. They're moving to some of the ghost towns themselves soon, to help the people there.

Maggie came to see me today. She's such a good friend that she rode her old bicycle instead of mine, in case I'd feel bad seeing it. Rags escaped from their yard again and went to our house on Oxford Street. I guess he can't understand why we left him behind. I feel so sorry for him. Maggie found him making his way back to her house looking very dejected!

And speaking of dejection, I told Maggie that Kay and Emma and I must leave Vancouver on Wednesday. She grabbed my hand and the two of us cried our eyes out. Maggie promised she'll come back to say goodbye. I asked her not to bring Rags because it would be too much for us both.

Monday, October 19

This morning my sisters and I learned where we're being sent — someplace called New Denver. We must be at the train station Wednesday morning with our belongings. Now we've got to decide which bags and parcels to take with us and which to leave for Mama and Papa. I'm trying hard not to be anxious. It's a good thing Kay and Emma are staying so calm and composed. Emma even remembered to write Tad and Mike so that they'll know where we're going!

Tuesday, October 20

Our last day in Vancouver. We STILL don't know where Papa is. Emma suspects his detention is connected with the upcoming big inquiry that's in all the papers. It's about the RCMP and the Security Commission's involvement with that shady Mr. Morii. Maybe they need Papa's help.

Meanwhile Mama is with Harry at the hospital. I wish my big brothers were with us. I'm really scared about what's going to happen once we leave.

But just like she promised, Maggie came to say goodbye after school. She even brought Ellen, Ida and her brother Len. I took pictures of everybody using my little camera. Maggie whispered that she'd say it belonged to her if any police or Mounties turned up. But none did.

We girls vowed to stay in touch. That reminded me of Sachi — I wondered when I'd see her again. Then I wondered if I would ever see *Maggie* again or Ellen or *anyone* in Vancouver. I started to feel terrible. But when it finally came time to say goodbye, Maggie had another great idea. We pretended it was one of our regular Guide meetings! It was only the Three Musketeers — Maggie, Ellen and me — but we recited the Guide promise and law together, just like always:

I promise, on my honour, to do my best:
To do my duty to God and the King,
To help other people at all times,
To obey the Guide Law.

A Guide's honour is to be trusted.
A Guide is loyal.
A Guide is useful and helps others.
A Guide is friend to all and a sister to every Guide.
A Guide is courteous.
A Guide is kind to animals and enjoys the beauty in nature.
A Guide obeys orders.
A Guide smiles and sings even under difficulty.
A Guide is thrifty.
A Guide is pure in thought, word and deed.

It was hard saying the words, but somehow it worked. I was sure I'd burst into tears when I hugged Maggie and Ellen goodbye. But they didn't cry, so I didn't either. I resolved I *would* do my best — even under difficulty, just like the Guide pledge says. I even feel a little bit better after writing it down now.

I'm making sure my camera is well hidden in my luggage. Luckily it's so small. I also carefully packed the album Geechan gave me with all my school and family photos. I took it out to look at one last time but Geechan's picture is at the front and it made me so sad again to see his face. There are photos of Tad and Mike and Rags in the album too, so I wrapped it up straight away. I'm remembering how brave Maggie and Ellen were when we said goodbye, so I won't cry now, not on the eve of our journey.

Wednesday, October 21

I'm writing on the train. We left Vancouver late this morning. Part of me was excited about my first train ride, but the other part was scared to be leaving. Mr. Young picked us up at the newspaper office and drove us to the station. It was really kind because we couldn't have managed all our bags without his help. My sisters each have two big suitcases plus several boxes. I have two small ones, which certainly feel as heavy as the bigger ones look!

My excitement disappeared when I saw so many sad looking families huddled with their belongings on the platform. They were mostly women and children, with a few elderly men who reminded me of Geechan again. I was glad he didn't have to go through this.

We waited forever before Kay and Emma's registration numbers were called. I don't have a card, so there was more confusion before the officials finally found my name listed with Mama and Papa's numbers. I don't know why they couldn't just use our names — we're *people,* not numbers!

The train finally arrived and we struggled getting our things on the baggage car. Then it was hard finding a place to sit together. An older lady moved so the three of us could share a bench and Kay said *"Arigatō gozaimasu"* to her. When we started moving, I was happy to be under way, but now I'm not sure. These hard wooden seats are so uncomfortable and there's nowhere we can even take a nap. I feel bad for the older people. I'm worried about Papa. And I miss Mama and Harry!

Later

Not much to see now — except trees and more trees. We still have a long way to go and it's getting dark. At least Emma packed a *bentō* with some *onigiri,* cold vegetables and a couple of apples, along with a thermos of green tea. I'll put this diary away now and catch up later.

〇

Thursday, October 22
Early morning

Still on the train. I've seen thousands of trees and quite a few mountains. The train ran right alongside a river a few times. We also crossed a couple of bridges and went into tunnels that passed right *through* mountains. I didn't like the total darkness! Someone said we should arrive in Slocan after noon.

Much later

The end of a *very* long day. We left Vancouver more than twenty-four hours ago. I can hardly keep my eyes open — we didn't sleep last night. When our train ride ended at Slocan City, we were brought here to New Denver in the back of a truck. Haven't seen much and it's dark now.

My sisters and I are in a rough wooden bunkhouse that reminds me of Guide Camp except it's a *lot* colder. There are beds for several people but we're the only ones here. There's no electricity so I'm using a flashlight Emma packed, so I can see while I write — she certainly knows what it means to be prepared!

I'm sleeping in my clothes tonight. I'm too tired to change and I don't think wearing pyjamas is such a good idea. I'll write more tomorrow.

ॐ

Friday, October 23

Woke up wondering where I was. Then I remembered and began to worry about Papa, Mama and Harry. But I decided I have to be brave like Maggie and Ellen.

Emma just called me. We're going to the mess hall to get breakfast and see New Denver in daylight. I'll write more later.

Much later

When we left the bunkhouse this morning, I couldn't believe my eyes. The scenery here is amazing! New Denver is right beside a big lake with huge mountains all around. Of course we have mountains in Vancouver, but here it feels like you can reach out and touch them. The one right across the lake even has a glacier!

But I should describe our arrival here. After we got to Slocan City yesterday afternoon, everyone tried to find their belongings in the heaps of luggage stacked on the platform. Younger children were crying. I thought of poor Harry and wondered how he is. I'm sure everyone was hungry, tired and worried about where they were going, like I was! Kay and Emma finally found our bags, then eventually we were told to get into the back of an old pickup truck that would take us to New Denver.

Other people travelled with us — a family with

a mother, three girls younger than me and an older lady who must have been the *baachan*. I remembered my Guide pledge and helped the girls onto the truck, while Kay and Emma did the same for the mother and grandmother. The *hakujin* driver said the old lady could sit in the cab, but she refused to be separated from her family. In the end, he put an older Japanese man on his own in the front and we finally drove off.

I felt sorry for Kay. When we left Vancouver, she wore her smartest outfit including her suede shoes. I bet she never dreamed she'd be riding in the back of a truck! It was mild back home, but there was snow in Slocan and at least a foot of it here. Kay's pretty shoes are ruined. It took ages to reach the village along a narrow winding road. We had to check in at the RCMP guardhouse before we finally stopped at the Security Commission building.

That's when we learned we must stay in the communal bunkhouse because our entire family isn't here yet. The Yamasakis — the people who shared our ride — were given a cabin together. The old man, Mr. Sato, has no family, and has to sleep in the men's bunkhouse. At least the driver took us to the mess hall, so we didn't have to carry our bags.

The mess is in an old hockey arena that's being used to serve meals now. One end is the men's bunkhouse. The women's is a separate building nearby. It was too late for a proper supper but someone gave us each a ham sandwich and a cup of tea. We ate quickly, then moved our bags to the bunkhouse and went to bed.

After breakfast today, we went exploring. Kay wore sturdier shoes this time! The main street has a few shops, a drugstore and a bank. There are some houses, a couple of churches, a post office and just one gas station. Bob's Ice Cream Parlour was closed — maybe it was too early for ice cream. But we didn't see a single bus, streetcar or even a traffic light. The roads here aren't even paved!

Emma wanted to ask about Papa and Mama and Harry, so we went back to the Commission offices. No one could tell us anything, so we left. We walked past an old-fashioned hotel and a rundown concert hall, and didn't see a soul anywhere. I see why New Denver is a ghost town!

Then we continued a mile south and crossed a small wooden bridge. Underneath is a noisy river, strangely called Carpenter Creek, rushing over thousands of small rocks. It isn't grand like the Lions Gate or Burrard Bridge back home, but I like being close to the water and hearing its sound. We've been told not to drink any because mining activities upstream make it unsafe.

We heard hammering as soon as we were over the bridge. I was astounded when we reached where the Japanese families are living. It's called "The Orchard," because there once was one here, and I spotted a few scruffy apple trees. But what a difference from the village! Here we saw rows and rows of little wooden cabins, some newly built and some still under construction. This must be like Lemon Creek where Sachi is. There are even a few sorry looking tents where people are still living — how awful. I'm very glad the Yamasakis got a cabin and I really hope the Yamadas have one by now. We could smell wood burning everywhere and see smoke rising from pipes on the cabin roofs. It reminds me a little of Guide Camp, except people at the mess said that no one here calls this place a camp because it's a reminder that we all were forced to come here.

At least this part of New Denver feels alive! People of all ages were coming and going, making me think of our visits to Powell Street or the crowd at an Asahi game. I didn't recognize anyone, but everyone smiled and said either hello or *ohayō*.

When we returned to the mess, Kay spotted a bulletin board outside. High-school students and graduates are needed to teach school here. Kay and Emma are going to apply because they don't think they could find other work. Maybe I'll be going to school after all!

Must stop now. It's cold, my hand is stiff and I'm really sleepy. I'm not looking forward to that cold bed one bit.

❧

Saturday, October 24

Woke up feeling terribly homesick. I wish I was back at Oxford Street! But if I can't be there, I want Mama and Papa to be here, and Harry and Mike and Tad too. I said the Guide pledge in my head and told myself to be brave. I felt a bit better when Emma said it was time to get up.

Hope we won't have to stay here long — it's freezing cold, dark and there's no running water. We have to bathe using water from the sinks in a small washroom at the mess. The cook said after all the cabins are built in The Orchard, the next priority is a communal *ofurō*. Mama and Aunt Eiko used one in Japan and had described it to us. I don't really want to take off all my clothes and be naked in front of a lot of strangers. Kay says the very idea is mortifying!

Sunday, October 25

Mike's here in New Denver!! I'm SO HAPPY to see him again. But I really should start from the beginning.

My sisters and I went to early mass this morning at St. Anthony's in the village, and ran into the Yamasakis there. The church is quite small and the pews were almost full, but the few *hakujin* sat well away from us. The priest is from Quebec and very welcoming — Mama would like him, I'm sure. I hope she and Harry get here soon! After mass, Father Clement greeted families outside and we introduced ourselves. None of the *hakujin* stayed. Then we walked back towards The Orchard with the Yamasakis. They invited us to their cabin for tea on Tuesday afternoon!

It was too early for lunch so Kay and Emma suggested we go see the "San." That's short for the sanitorium, the new hospital for tuberculosis patients being built south of The Orchard. We walked that way, heading for a pretty little cove with a wide, pebbly beach. Loud hammering was coming from a long, wooden building even though it was Sunday. Several men were hard at work. Suddenly one of them whistled and ran towards us. It was Mike!

He reached me first, picked me up and spun me around. I was so overjoyed to see him, I burst into tears! He hugged us all and wanted to know what we were doing here. We asked the same of him, since his last letter said he was someplace called Sandon!

He laughed and said that Sandon is another ghost town near here. He was there several months, getting the old buildings ready for evacuees. Afterwards, he and the other workers came here to complete the San before really bad weather sets in.

Mike didn't know we'd turn up here. Emma's last letter didn't reach him. We said we'd just arrived late Thursday night. He asked right away where Mama and Papa and Harry are. He knew Tad was in Ontario because he did get one of Emma's earlier letters, as well as the one with the bad news about Geechan. We told Mike that Harry was in St. Paul's Hospital when we left Vancouver and Mama was with him. When Kay said that Papa had been detained by the RCMP two weeks ago and that we hadn't heard from him since, Mike muttered, "Damn it!" I've *never* heard him swear before!

Emma explained that she'd been trying to find out where Papa is and when we might see him. She's trying to reach Aunt Eiko to see if she can help. When Mike learned Aunt Eiko is in Kaslo and working for the Commission, he looked surprised, but said it can only help to know somebody in the Commission office. He laughed again when we told him where we're staying. He's sleeping at the men's bunkhouse right next door. We're going to meet for supper tonight at the mess hall!

Monday, October 26
At the mess hall

It's better writing here than in the bunkhouse with a flashlight! Supper with Mike last night was wonderful. Having him here helps me worry a bit less about Papa, Mama and Harry. Mike said he had to work really hard at the road camp. He was terribly homesick those first weeks and not just for Mama's cooking. That's exactly how I'm feeling now! The other workers were mostly older men who didn't speak or write much English. When he wasn't at work clearing bush, Mike would write letters to the Commission for the men because they desperately wanted to rejoin their families.

In May, Mike was sent to Kaslo to fix up old buildings there for the evacuees. Being in Kaslo was better than road camp because more men Mike's age were working there. He even knew a few from the lumberyard. After that, Mike and his friends were sent to Sandon, set in a narrow valley between here and Kaslo. The main street is a wooden boardwalk built right over Carpenter Creek, the same river that ends up here in New Denver. Mike told us the town had five thousand people in its boom years but when he and the others arrived, only a few dozen remained. Nearly a thousand Japanese Canadians live there now.

In one of the old hotel dining rooms, Mike saw plates of untouched food still on the tables, as if people left in the middle of eating and were coming back any moment. A Sandon old-timer later told him that when residents found out the Japanese were coming there to live, most packed their bags and took the first bus out of town!

We left the mess hall late, but at least there's no curfew here! We said goodnight and headed off to our separate bunkhouses. It feels so good to be together, even if it's just the four of us. If only we were *all* together — Tad and Papa, and Mama and Harry too.

Tuesday, October 27

Kay and Emma went to a meeting about the teaching jobs after breakfast, so I was on my own. I took a long walk along the main road until there were no more houses. The only traffic was a big truck loaded with logs. I noticed a sign to Rosebery, another internment camp north of here, and another sign pointing east to Sandon and Kaslo. I kept going as far as the railway tracks and nearly jumped out of my skin when a boy my age suddenly appeared and asked if I was lost!

I told him I wasn't. Then he asked me whether I was from Rosebery or The Orchard, because if I was from Rosebery, it was faster following the tracks than using the main road. I thanked him and said I was from The Orchard, even though that's not entirely true! He smiled and said he might see me there. His father is one of the Doukhobor farmers in the area who sell vegetables to the Japanese. They're usually at The Orchard on Thursdays.

The boy's name is Alex Davidoff. He likes walking the tracks because he often sees birds and deer. We headed back to the road together just as a bearded man in a horse-drawn wagon pulled up. Alex said it was his father and went to meet him. But before he did, he tipped his cap and wished me good day! I waved as the wagon went by and Alex waved back. It's strange he wasn't in school.

After lunch, my sisters and I went to visit the

Yamasakis. I was stunned when we went inside but tried not to show it. It's tiny, yet Mrs. Yamasaki said it's really a two-family cabin. There's no electricity and no running water here either. The wooden kitchen sink has a hole that drains straight outside!

Mrs. Yamasaki sent her daughters to fetch water for tea so I went along to help. It's quite a distance to the village. The full buckets were very heavy but Mrs. Yamasaki gave the youngest girl a metal teapot to carry instead. Now I understand why Sachi wrote that this was such hard work.

The girls are so polite, not *yancha* like Harry. Dori is nine, Joy is seven and Bonnie is five. The older lady, Mrs. Imai, is Mrs. Yamasaki's mother and the girls' *baachan*. Mr. Yamasaki owned a Vancouver dry cleaning shop, but like Mas, he was sent to Angler for protesting back in May. His family hasn't had a letter from him since September.

The cabin has two wood stoves, one for heating and one for cooking. My sisters helped Mrs. Yamasaki start the fire in the cooking stove because she was so used to her electric stove in Vancouver. The *ocha* was good and Mrs. Imai brought out a tin of *senbei* to munch on. Mrs. Yamasaki apologized for not having any nice teacups but, like everyone else, the family left their good dishes behind at home. We had a nice visit all the same and made some new friends. And I think I may have made friends with a Doukhobor today too!

Wednesday, October 28

It snowed last night! It's pretty but harder to get around. Once Mama gets here, which I hope is soon, Kay said we'll order boots from Eaton's catalogue. We're going to need long johns too!

Today Emma went to the Commission office again, trying to discover when the rest of our family is coming here. She's been as worried as Kay and I are about our parents and Harry, and she wants to see Aunt Eiko. A bus runs to Kaslo but Emma needs a permit to travel. The Mountie stationed here, Corporal Sayers, told Emma he has business in Kaslo on Friday and offered to drive her there. When Emma asked about the permit, Corporal Sayers said he'd overlook it this one time!!

Thursday, October 29

A letter from Mama today at last! She's leaving Vancouver soon and coming here with Harry. He's had bronchitis but is over the worst of it. What a relief to finally know he's okay. But Mama still has no news about Papa. I hope and pray he's safe and not in a prisoner-of-war camp. I can't help thinking about when we didn't get any news about Geechan for such a long time. But I'm going to try to be brave and not worry.

I walked to The Orchard this morning to see if Alex might be there. Several horse-drawn wagons were in the clearing by the road. Some farmers had their children with them. The Japanese were buying carrots, cabbages, potatoes and other vegetables. Alex was helping his father and I went over to say hello. He gave me an apple!

Later I asked Emma why the Doukhobor children weren't in school. She said their parents believe in home-schooling. It's strange how we *can't* go to school but the Doukhobor children *don't*.

Next Monday, Kay, Emma and other girls hoping to teach are meeting a lady named Hide Hyodo. Everyone knows about her because she was one of the four people who went to Ottawa to try and get us the vote. She's also the first Japanese person in B.C. to become a teacher. Children in the camps aren't allowed to attend any local schools, but their parents complained so much that the Security Commission hired Miss Hyodo to set up schools for grades one to eight. The higher grades have to wait until next year, but I might be going to school after all — at least if we have to stay here that long!

Kay and Emma are excited about teaching. I miss school and my friends even more. I wonder if Sachi misses me as much as I do her. I hope I hear from her soon, as well as Maggie and Ellen. The gang can't be the same without us — just two Musketeers!

At least Mama and Harry will be here before long. And I hope and pray Papa will be too. I'm anxious about him most of all.

Friday, October 30

Corporal Sayers drove Emma to Kaslo and back! He was picking up Miss Hyodo for next week's meeting here. Emma got to see Aunt Eiko, who knew that Mama and Harry are coming to New Denver next week, but STILL had no news about Papa for us. I'm trying really hard not to worry about him, or that's all I'll do.

Emma says Miss Hyodo is really nice and is going to live in New Denver while she sets up the different schools. While Emma was in Kaslo, Kay and I visited Cash & Service, the dry goods store. They've started carrying products we need, like candles, fabric and sewing supplies. Even the grocery store is supposed to get Japanese food soon.

Sunday, November 1

We move to a cabin tomorrow! Maybe the Commission finally heard Emma's complaints. We'll have to share with another family, but it will be nice to be warm again. If only there was indoor plumbing too!

Monday, November 2

Kay and Emma spent most of today at the meeting with Miss Hyodo. She's interviewing girls to decide which grade they will teach. The new schools are using the same curriculum as regular schools back home. It's strange to think of my sisters as teachers, but I'm sure they'll be good ones.

Tuesday, November 3

We moved in with the Yamasakis yesterday! They're happy we're joining their little household for a short time, even the *baachan*.

The cabin was crowded already with five people and their belongings, and now there are three more. With just two bedrooms, Dori must share ours since there are only two bunk beds in each one. The girls were so curious when we arrived. Mrs. Yamasaki asked them to keep out of our way, but there's nowhere for them to go. At home I used to complain about sharing with my two sisters. Now there are *four* of us in this much smaller room!

It's so nice of Mrs. Yamasaki to have us eat with their family, since our dishes and cooking things are still with Mama. To help with the expenses, my sisters and I went to the village grocery store for some food. A lady was asking the price of a bag of onions. When the clerk said, "Fifty cents," she exclaimed, "But it was just a dime in Vancouver last month!" He replied, "Well, there's a war on." Emma gave him the look and said it was highway robbery, but he just shrugged. I don't know if that lady bought the onions or not, but we had to. Kay handed over five one-dollar bills for our shopping and only got a few cents change. Next time we should get our vegetables from the Doukhobors!

We had supper tonight by candlelight and the food was much better than at the mess. Mrs. Yamasaki invited Mike to join us. He said how wonderful it was to have home cooking again — beef *okazu*, rice, pickles and *miso* soup. Mrs. Imai had wisely packed a lot of Japanese food staples.

After we ate, Mike said goodnight and went back to his bunkhouse. Kay and Emma did the dishes. I read the little girls a story from my fairy-tale book before they said their prayers and went to bed. Now I'm writing here at the kitchen table — its rough boards make my writing bumpy.

It's still cold in here and not much better than the bunkhouse. Being around the Yamasakis makes me miss the rest of my family more than ever. I'll run to the outhouse before I go to bed. I'm going to sleep in my clothes again!

Wednesday, November 4

Woke up early feeling sad, wondering when I'll ever see Papa again. I would have stayed in bed but it's freezing! It must be worse for those people still living in those wretched tents. Our little bedroom window is all frosted over. I can hear Mrs. Yamasaki and Mrs. Imai up already, filling the heating stove with wood. Dori is awake now too. I see her peeking out from under the covers on the top bunk across from me. I'll stop writing now and get up.

Later

Mrs. Yamasaki did laundry after breakfast. It's so much work without a wringer washer! At least we can use lake water for this. After the girls and I got some, Mrs. Yamasaki heated it on the stove and poured it over the dirty clothes in a metal tub. She scrubbed everything on a washboard with a bar of yellow soap, dumped the water outside and rinsed everything in fresh water. We all helped wring the clothes as dry as possible. The clean washing had to be hung up inside the cabin because it would freeze outside! Mrs. Yamasaki apologized for the disruption this morning, but at least my sisters and I learned what's involved. I'll need clean clothes soon and doing laundry won't be fun, especially in such cramped quarters.

Thursday, November 5

I told Mrs. Yamasaki and my sisters that we should get our vegetables from the Doukhobors. After breakfast we all walked over to the clearing by the road. I took them over to the Davidoffs' wagon, so I could meet Alex again. He waved when he saw me and I introduced him to everyone. The prices were much better than the grocery store. Kay got a big basket of apples for a dime and tonight she and Emma made a pie. They used coupons from our ration books to buy sugar in the village.

The girls and I had to go back to the village to get more water for cooking and doing dishes. What a nuisance!

Friday, November 6

Emma mailed Tad a letter at the post office and brought back one for me from Maggie! It's so good to hear from her. She and Ellen miss me and Sachi a lot, especially at Guide meetings and grass hockey. Rags is fine and Ida is taking good care of him. They've had more air-raid drills at school and Templeton has new equipment — shovels and buckets of sand to put out fires in case of bombs. I must write and tell Maggie about everything that's happened to me so far. I'll write Sachi too, so she'll know where I am. I wonder how much her camp is like ours?

This afternoon Mike taught Kay, Emma and Mrs. Yamasaki how to split logs! He wants them to be able to do it if he's not around. The Commission workers like Mike's friend Johnny Takenaka bring us more wood every week, but we use it so quickly, just like everyone else here.

Saturday, November 7

While my sisters were at the Commission office this morning, trying to get news about Mama and Harry, Mrs. Yamasaki helped her daughters bathe.

She heated lots of fresh water on the stove and poured it in the washtub. The little girls went first. Then I bathed too, while everyone else stayed in the bedrooms.

Of course, we had to get *more* water this afternoon so Mrs. Yamasaki, Mrs. Imai, and Kay and Emma could bathe. Mrs. Imai is looking forward to the *ofurō* being built, but public bathing still doesn't appeal to me!

Monday, November 9

No time to write before bedtime last night, so I'm scribbling this at breakfast today. Mama and Harry arrived yesterday! They left Vancouver Saturday on a special hospital train. Corporal Sayers picked them up in Slocan and brought them to the Newmarket Hotel in the village.

The moment the car pulled up, I flung open the passenger door and hugged Mama so hard her hat fell off! I blurted out that Mike was here in New Denver too. Mama was very surprised and happy. Harry scrambled out of the car and Kay and Emma gave him big hugs. So did I. He was a little pale, but looked pretty good for someone who's been ill so long.

And Emma never said how handsome Corporal Sayers is! He carried Mama's suitcases into the hotel foyer for her. Kay said, "Thank you very much, Corporal," and he blushed. My big sister is a flirt!

The Newmarket isn't like hotels back home. Papa, Harry and I once waited outside the Hotel Vancouver, just after it was built, to see King George and Queen Elizabeth when they toured Canada. It's a grand skyscraper but the Newmarket is just an old three-storey building made of wood. The San isn't ready or Harry might have gone there instead. At least this hotel has real beds and electric lights. There's even a bathtub, so I asked Mama if I could have a bath sometime soon. She laughed because both Kay and Emma had already asked the same thing! She promised we could all have baths another time. Mama just wanted to eat something, get Harry to bed and go to bed herself!

That's when Emma unwrapped the *furoshiki* she'd brought. It was a *bentō* Mrs. Yamasaki and her mother had made for Mama and Harry. Mama asked us to thank Mrs. Yamasaki and Mrs. Imai for their kindness, which we did when we returned to the cabin.

Later

Our turn for laundry this morning. My sisters wanted it done before we went to see Mama and Harry. Such a lot of hard work! We hung our clothes up, hoping they'll be dry by the time we go to bed tonight. Thank goodness there are no men or boys living in the cabin with our underwear hanging in plain view!

Tuesday, November 10

Mama finally had news of Papa! Somehow Aunt Eiko tracked him down at last. He was released from detention in Vancouver but then was sent to Tashme, an internment camp near the town of Hope! The Commission mixed him up with another Kobayashi family living there instead of sending him here. Aunt Eiko doesn't know how soon he can join us, but at least we know he's safe. Mama's still worried about him and I am too, but at least we know he hasn't been sent to Ontario. I was so afraid he might have ended up in that prisoner-of-war camp like the Nakagawas' son Mas!

Several families left The Orchard for new cabins at Harris Ranch, another camp nearby. Their old homes are being used for the new school. Some of Mike's friends are taking down the inside walls. Miss Hyodo wants classes to begin as soon as possible. Kay and Emma say it's a disgrace that some families are STILL living in tents.

Wednesday, November 11

It's Remembrance Day. We went for a walk in the village and someone had put a wreath on the cenotaph near the lake. I wonder if anyone will do the same for the memorial in Stanley Park now that all the Japanese veterans have left Vancouver.

Thursday, November 12

I saw Alex again this morning. Mrs. Yamasaki bought more vegetables and Kay got another basket of apples. The pie was a big hit last week!

I had a letter from Sachi today — it's nearly two months old! But it's wonderful to hear from her. I'm pasting her letter in here.

September 14, 1942

Dear Mary,

I hope this letter finds you well. I'm sorry I haven't written sooner but life here in Lemon Creek is so different from Vancouver.

I admit I was angry when I had to leave our home and my best friends. There isn't even a school here I can go to! That seemed worse than not having running water or electricity and having to live in this tent. We've been promised we'll have a cabin soon.

But I'm so busy helping my parents and looking after my younger brother and sister, I can't complain. You know me, I'm an optimist! It's very beautiful here in the mountains and I've been picking berries and mushrooms like we learned at Guide Camp. I miss you and Maggie and Ellen but I just know I'll see you again somehow and that we

Musketeers will be reunited someday. Please
say hello to everyone in your family for me.

Affectionately,
Sachi

Sunday, November 15

It poured yesterday so we were stuck inside all day. At least we didn't have to fetch water. But we needed an umbrella to use the outhouse!

And more rain today. Mama didn't think Harry should go to church yet. She's being extra careful that he doesn't get sick again. Emma and Kay and I went to mass with the Yamasakis and our shoes are a mucky mess.

Thursday, November 19

Maggie sent me another letter! She says that she forgot to tell me that Billy Foster is in Ellen's class this year. He got a detention for calling Edith Brady "four-eyed" because she wears glasses. I guess there aren't any more Japanese kids for him to pick on now.

And Maggie says the grass-hockey team lost three games in a row without me and Sachi.

It's so UNFAIR that I can't be with my best friends. But there's nothing I can do about it, so I'll try to be more positive like Sachi.

Sunday, November 22

Mama and Harry came to St. Anthony's this morning and finally met the Yamasakis. It was Harry's first real outing since he arrived here. Afterwards, Mrs. Yamasaki invited Mama and Harry for tea, so everyone came back to the cabin. Harry's eyes almost popped out of his head when he got inside, but he didn't say anything rude, thank goodness. He did eat more than his fair share of *senbei,* though! At first the girls were shy around Harry, but they played *Jan-Ken-Pon* and were soon laughing together. And Bonnie beat Harry twice!

Tuesday, November 24

Dr. Uchida, the camp doctor, checked Harry out today. His lungs are clear and he should be fine to live in a cabin with the rest of us. That's good news!

Thursday, November 26

This morning Alex said it's going to snow soon. At least all the people living in tents finally have their cabins.

We had a letter from Tad today, addressed to us here, so he knows we're in New Denver. He's driving a truck in Toronto now. The pay isn't great, but it's better than Commission wages. And he says people in Toronto are very friendly. I'm glad to hear that, because the village of Silverton, south of here, wanted to put up a barrier on the main road to keep us out. I just don't understand why some people hate us so much!

Sunday, November 29

Papa's here and we're finally all together! Except for Tad and of course Geechan. Papa was at last permitted to leave Tashme. He got here late yesterday afternoon. All of us anxiously waited at the village gas station. It's been so long since we've seen him that I didn't think I could stand waiting even one more second.

When Papa stepped out of Johnny Takenaka's truck, he was surrounded! We'd never seen him hug Mama before but he held her tight until tears ran down her cheeks. Then he hugged each of us. We all cried because we're so happy, even Mike!

I can admit in these pages that I was really afraid we might never see Papa again. He was very tired from his long trip, so we didn't ask him too many questions. He's spending the night with Mama and Harry, but said it would be the last time he'd leave us. I'm saying lots of thankful prayers tonight now that Papa is back with us again!

Monday, November 30

Too busy to write — my sisters and I have to move again. But our family is going to be *together*. The Commission is finding us our own cabin.

Wednesday, December 2

We left New Denver for Rosebery. This morning Johnny helped us move all our things here. He sure spends a lot of time helping us lately. I think he's sweet on Kay — someone else besides Corporal Sayers!

We said goodbye to the Yamasakis this morning. Mrs. Yamasaki gave me a little present for helping with her daughters, a heart-shaped *origami* bookmark. I wasn't much help, really — we were only with them for a month — but she insisted! I hope someone nice will share the Yamasakis' cabin now that we're leaving.

Johnny drove Papa, Mama and Harry from the hotel. Mike is staying at the bunkhouse until the San is finished. The rest of us took the shortcut along the railway tracks Alex told me about. Now I see why he likes this route. There are big trees everywhere and it's so quiet! We saw several different paw prints in the snow beside the tracks. I hope none belonged to bears!

Rosebery is smaller than The Orchard but is also right beside the lake. Our new home is exactly like the Yamasakis'. There's still no electricity or running water but we don't have to walk as far for fresh water. I hoped we wouldn't have to use outhouses here, but I'm wrong. And that bath I had at the hotel last week may be my last real one for a while. Johnny got the heating stove going, but it's as cold here as anywhere else we've stayed. Poor Harry is finally getting better and now he has to live *here*. But I shouldn't complain. We're together at last. That's all that really matters!

Saturday, December 5

We've spent the past two days making our cabin as comfortable and convenient as possible. We're lucky to have our own place — perhaps because we were one of the last families to arrive here. Most others share two families to a cabin like we did with the Yamasakis.

Papa put up some shelves in the kitchen for our cups and plates and cooking supplies. Mike can build more shelving for us in the bedrooms later. Kay and Emma helped Mama unpack most of our bags and organized our things so we can find what we need, like warm clothing, right away. Mama even has her sewing machine in a corner.

But Kay is moving back to New Denver next week to teach. She'll live in a house provided by the Commission. And now that Emma's in Rosebery, she'll be teaching school here instead of at The Orchard. Miss Hyodo was here yesterday making sure the classrooms will be ready soon.

Sunday, December 6

There's no church here, so my sisters and I dressed warmly and left early this morning for mass at St. Anthony's. We took the shortcut again but Johnny picked up the rest of our family later and drove them to the church, where we all met up. After mass we introduced Papa to the Yamasakis. He thanked Mrs. Yamasaki for being so good to us while he and Mama weren't here. Mrs. Yamasaki looked happy because she finally received a letter from her husband!

Johnny took Mama, Papa and Harry home in the truck but the rest of us walked back. It's so peaceful, at least when there are no trains!

Monday, December 7

We've been using up our supply of candles, so I'll just write a bit before heading to bed. Everybody has been complaining about the lack of good lighting, so Johnny said we're all getting oil lamps soon. (We could really use an extra heating stove too.) I still wear my clothes to bed every night. I'm also using one of the hot water bottles Mama brought from Oxford Street — this morning we had frost on the blankets, not just the windows.

Papa mentioned that today was the first anniversary of Pearl Harbor. It's hard to believe all that's happened to our family and our community since then. I wonder what next year will bring.

Tuesday, December 8

Alex and his father came to Rosebery with some other farmers today. I thanked him for his advice about the shortcut. He promised to show me good places to pick huckleberries next summer. I may actually use some of the things I learned in Guide Camp about foraging! But with all the snow here, summer seems such a long time away.

Mama bought lots of vegetables and wrapped them in the old newspapers we'd used to pack our kitchen things. She put them in a cardboard box near the door. Without a refrigerator, we keep any perishables in a crate outside, underneath the cabin, but have to be careful they don't freeze. Too bad Rags isn't here to scare away any bears or wolves!

Thursday, December 10

Johnny brought us a coal oil lamp today. Everyone has one now. The cabin is so much brighter at night. Mama says the lamp is a lot better for sewing — candlelight was very hard on her eyes. She's making us flannel shirts and blouses. Emma unravelled an old wool sweater and is knitting Harry socks.

I've written to Maggie again and Johnny mailed my letter. I hope she'll get it by Christmas!

Saturday, December 12

When I was fetching water this morning, I met a nice girl named Nora Hisaki. Her family's been here since September. They had a farm on the Island and spent three months in Hastings Park before coming to New Denver. Then they lived in one of those miserable tents in The Orchard until they finally got their cabin here.

Sunday, December 13

Cold and snowy today. We didn't go to church. Mama said she's sure God won't hold it against us. I hope she's right. Harry and I had fun building a snowman outside of our cabin. We used twigs to make his face because Mama didn't want to let us use any of her carrots for a nose!

Monday, December 14

Kay has gone back to New Denver. Johnny (of course!) took her things to the house where she's staying with four other teachers. I'm jealous because they surely have electricity and indoor plumbing. It must be warmer than our cabin! But I'm going to miss my big sister now that she's left us again.

Emma's been busy preparing her lessons. The classroom cabins finally were finished here today, so school opens tomorrow!

Tuesday, December 15

School started here today. I'm disappointed it only goes to Grade Eight, but Emma asked me to be her unofficial helper today, since I can't go to school myself.

Emma's teaching Grades Three and Four. She has twenty-five students including Harry and two of Nora's sisters. Everyone must *always* speak English in class because the Commission forbids any Japanese. Desks and books have to be shared since there aren't enough to go around. But all the children seem glad to be here instead of being stuck in their cabins.

Emma told her class they've missed so much school already, they must work really hard to catch up. She began reviewing Vocabulary and Arithmetic and even gave out homework on the first day! While Emma taught a Grade Four lesson, I made sure the Grade Three kids worked on the exercises she had given them. Harry didn't want any help from me! I also kept the heating stove stocked with wood, a chore that needs a lot of attention. Class was over at one o'clock and I was surprised how quickly the time passed. I missed Alex today but I'll probably see him again.

Wednesday, December 16

Today was the second day of school but Emma didn't need me. I asked Nora over to our cabin since her four younger sisters were all at school. She asked me what it was like growing up in Vancouver, so I told her about our home on Oxford Street, about Maggie and Sachi and Ellen, about going to Templeton and Girl Guides, about Rags and even Geechan. I suddenly felt so homesick, I burst into tears!

Nora hugged me and gave me her handkerchief. She said she missed her home on their farm too, her friends at school and living on the Island. Her family had two dogs and two cats they had to give up! Whenever I feel sorry for myself, I should remember that everyone here has lost their homes and so much more.

Thursday, December 17

Nora and I spent the morning searching for kindling. We need every little bit! We found some driftwood near the lake and some pine cones under the snow. We even used the twigs from Harry's snowman.

Nora told her mother about Mama's sewing machine, so Mrs. Hisaki asked Mama if she could mend some of her daughters' clothes. Mama was delighted! She says it makes her feel useful again.

Saturday, December 19

Kay visited us today. Johnny drove her over and also brought some groceries Mama couldn't get at the little store here. School started in The Orchard yesterday and Kay's teaching Grade Eight. She says her classroom isn't any warmer than Emma's — the ink bottles were frozen solid when her students arrived for class! She and Emma talked on and on about teaching, as if I wasn't even there. And I was wrong about the house Kay and her teacher friends are living in just outside New Denver. It's so old the plumbing doesn't work and they still have to use outhouses!

Sunday, December 20

No church again today. Mama said she'd rather try to go at Christmas.

Tuesday, December 22

I saw Alex this morning and introduced him to Nora. She says he's a nice boy but thinks his father's bushy beard is scary! I wished Alex a Merry Christmas and gave him an *origami* crane I'd folded from some nice paper I've been saving. He wished me a Merry Christmas too and gave me another apple he polished on his sleeve!

Wednesday, December 23

Last day of school before Christmas. Classes will still be held next week, though. Emma's determined her pupils will catch up on their school year.

There's a full moon over the lake tonight. And I heard something howling in the distance when I dashed to the outhouse. Papa put the bacon we're keeping under the cabin in a big *senbei* tin to make sure we don't attract any unwanted animals!!

Friday, December 25

Yesterday Harry and I had naps so we could go to midnight mass. Corporal Sayers picked the five of us up and drove us to St. Anthony's, where we met Mike and Kay.

It was good being with most of my family again, but I prayed for my friends and relatives scattered all over. I'm not sure Buddhists go to heaven but I prayed for Geechan anyway. After his sermon, Father Clement wished us peace and joy and that's what I really felt this year.

And now it's Christmas. Our little cabin is a long way from Oxford Street, but Kay and Mike stayed overnight so we'd be together.

We lost so much in the past year. Our home, our friends, our dog, our belongings, Geechan. But I'm so grateful because Papa is finally back with us and safe.

1943

Friday, January 1

A quiet New Year's Day. Mike and Kay stayed in New Denver with their friends. Harry and I read books all afternoon. Emma kept busy preparing her lessons, Mama sewed and Papa fixed the kitchen shelf that fell down on Boxing Day. It started snowing again this afternoon. I hope this new year will be a good one! It can't be worse than last year.

Sunday, January 3

Too much snow to go to St. Anthony's today, so I said a prayer of thanks to have most of my family back.

Wednesday, January 13

Last Wednesday there even was MORE snow. I need some new books to read. And I'll need a new diary soon — not much room left here to write.

The Rosebery store is running low on supplies. The snow let up a bit, so Papa and I walked to New Denver yesterday to visit the shops for food — not much selection there either.

But more snow today — several inches. Emma finally had to close the school. It's so cold and there's not even enough wood for everyone's heating stoves. And it's harder than ever to fetch water!

Thursday, January 14

Snow and more snow. Another FOOT fell today. We could barely get out of our cabin this morning, even to visit the outhouse! It's colder than ever and tonight we're all huddled around the stoves. We're using up all our wood, so we hope Johnny brings more soon!

Sunday, January 17

Couldn't get to church. The road to New Denver is blocked off. Harry and I stumbled down to the lake, looking for driftwood. Everybody else must have had the same idea because we didn't find any.

Vancouver was NEVER this cold and snowy. How on earth does the Commission expect us to keep warm here?

Friday, January 22

It's so cold the water pipe's frozen. We've got to melt snow for water or else break the ice to get some from the lake. Every morning now we wake up to frost on the blankets. It's like living in another century! I hate being a pioneer.

We're running low on vegetables and meat too. And there's no mail either — Johnny said the road's completely snowed in between New Denver and Kaslo. He's been busy rounding up young men and teenage boys to work at the sawmill because wood is desperately needed. That's where Mike and his friends have gone now.

Sunday, January 24

Porridge for supper tonight.

Monday, January 25

Porridge again, for breakfast and supper. For lunch, Mama made *okayu* with leftover cold rice. If the snow doesn't stop soon, we won't have *any* food left. And we're running low on wood again. There's no more room to write here. Maybe I should burn this diary for fuel! Last year was so terrible, it may help me forget what happened to us.

But I should remember my Guide pledge and "smile under difficulty." I'll try my best to be like Sachi and think positively.

Geechan would expect that of me.

Epilogue

❧

Mary did not burn her diary after all. Emma was able to persuade her to keep it to remember the good things that happened, as well as the bad.

Although the winter of 1942–43 was one of the worst ever in the Slocan Valley, the snow and cold gradually stopped. By the end of February, the schools in Rosebery and New Denver reopened. Spring arrived and families put in gardens and spent more time outdoors. Mary's father used some of Geechan's seeds he'd saved from Oxford Street. More people brought Mrs. Kobayashi sewing jobs. Mary's sisters worked well into July to make up for their students' lost time. And even while busy teaching, Emma completed her senior matriculation through correspondence courses.

In June, taps were installed throughout The Orchard, one for each group of eight or nine cabins, so the Yamasakis didn't have to walk to the village for water anymore. Eventually, cold water was piped right into all the cabins in the Slocan camps. The Orchard's *ofurō* was built, though Mary and her sisters detested using it. Electricity came to the cabins in the fall of 1943, much to Mrs. Kobayashi's delight. Movies, concerts, bazaars and school presentations took place at New Denver's old Bosun

Hall. Mike's gramophone and records were finally put to good use at the dances held there.

Harry thrived and didn't fall sick during those hard winter months. He enjoyed school, made new friends and learned to swim in Slocan Lake. Mary and Nora took Emma's advice and did Grade Nine correspondence courses, but were still able to swim, hike and explore their beautiful surroundings. Mary used her camera regularly, but Corporal Sayers never did a thing about it! She used her Guide training to pick fiddleheads in the spring, berries in summer and mushrooms with her father in the fall. She and Nora made numerous friends among the many young people living in the camps.

Throughout spring and summer, the gardens flourished and the community no longer relied on the Doukhobors to supplement their food supply. Mary did not see Alex regularly anymore. But she did meet him once more that summer on the shortcut between Rosebery and New Denver. He kept his promise and showed her the best spots for picking huckleberries.

In August Mr. Kobayashi found a job at the drugstore in New Denver and the family moved again to a real house in town. Mary was thrilled to have indoor plumbing again! In September Emma joined Kay as a teacher in The Orchard while Mary and Nora started Grade Ten at the newly opened Notre Dame High School in the village.

The following winter, cabins were insulated

with tarpaper and cedar shakes to keep out the cold and drafts, but the previous year's harsh weather did not reoccur. Electricity and piped-in water made life easier. And the shops were well stocked with Japanese food.

In Toronto, Tad tried to enlist again — without success. He continued to drive a truck delivering newspapers, and wrote frequently to persuade his family to come east. Early in 1944, Mike was the first to leave New Denver, since Japanese Canadians were encouraged to depart if they could find employment outside B.C. He and Johnny moved into the same Toronto boarding house as Tad; both quickly found work.

In the summer of 1944, Kay and Emma also left for Toronto. Kay worked as a seamstress in a dress shop owned by a Jewish family, while Emma became a maid for a wealthy couple in Rosedale. The Jewish community often helped displaced Japanese Canadians from B.C. by offering them work or finding them places to live. Emma applied to nursing school and when she was accepted that fall, she began her studies in earnest.

In January 1945, Ottawa finally allowed a limited number of Japanese Canadians to join the army as translators. Tad, Mike and Johnny immediately signed up to begin basic training in Brantford, Ontario. That summer they returned to Vancouver for additional instruction in the Canadian Intelligence Corps. But before they were sent overseas, the United

States dropped an atomic bomb on the Japanese city of Hiroshima on August 6, killing at least one hundred thousand people. A second bomb fell on the city of Nagasaki on August 9, killing about seventy thousand more. Mary was saddened to realize that many of Geechan's family still living there would not have survived. Japan surrendered on September 2. While a few *Nisei* reached southeast Asia before that, the army dismissed the remaining recruits the following year.

Mr. and Mrs. Kobayashi, Mary and Harry left New Denver in August 1945. With the help of money that Tad, Mike and Kay had saved, Mr. Kobayashi bought a house in Toronto. Its yards were smaller than Oxford Street and Mary's room had no mountain view, but it soon became home. Mary began Grade Twelve in September and eventually graduated from the University of Toronto with a degree in English Literature. Inspired by her sisters' dedication in the camps, she too became a teacher. She later married Bob Endo, whom she'd met in New Denver, and had two daughters.

Tad, Mike and Johnny returned to Toronto in August 1946. Soon after, Kay married Johnny; they had three sons. Emma achieved her dream and became a nurse at Toronto's St. Joseph's Hospital. Harry finished high school, then graduated from the University of Toronto's Forestry program and found a job with a lumber company. He was the only Kobayashi to return to Vancouver, where he married and had five children.

Sachi and her family also moved to Toronto after the war. She and Mary saw each other at least once a year. They seldom talked about the internment years, but often reminisced about Maggie, Ellen, Girl Guides and Oxford Street, as well as tennis and Revels and Rags.

Maggie became a teacher like Mary, until she married and had five children. Despite her busy life she wrote Mary regularly. In 1984 she and Ellen flew to Toronto for an emotional reunion with Mary and Sachi.

Two years later Mary returned to Vancouver for the first time since 1942. Harry took her to see what was left of their old neighbourhood. 2321 Oxford Street had been sold in 1943 and was torn down, along with several other homes in the block, including Sachi's. An apartment building now stood in their place. The furniture that the families had left behind and the special things they'd stored in their attics had all been lost long ago.

But the Girls' Day dolls and Boys' Day banners that Mary's mother had shipped to her sister in Montreal were returned to the family after the war. Mrs. Kobayashi gave the Boys' Day banners to Tad when his first son was born, and the Girls' Day dolls to Mary when she had her first daughter.

Mr. Kobayashi worked in several drugstores

until his retirement in 1965. Mrs. Kobayashi continued to do sewing work as long as she lived.

On March 31, 1949, Japanese Canadians were finally allowed to vote in federal elections anywhere in Canada. Mr. and Mrs. Kobayashi lined up at their local municipal polling station in the first election in which they could vote. They made sure to cast their ballots in every election after that — municipal, provincial or federal — for the rest of their lives. In 1988 the entire Kobayashi family went to Ottawa to march on Parliament Hill in support of the redress movement that sought an apology from the government for the injustices against Japanese Canadians during the war.

Historical Note

The Early Years

British Columbia in the 1800s was vast and largely undeveloped. But by the first half of the twentieth century, the province was growing and prospering with the help of large groups of immigrants from China, Japan and India. Yet B.C. remained British to the core. The majority of the population was white and Anglo-Saxon, and those in power — politicians and business owners — strongly disliked any minorities who were not.

The first official immigrant from Japan came to B.C. in 1877; many more arrived in the following years. In Vancouver, several Japanese-owned stores and boarding houses opened near Hastings Mill and around Powell Street. By the 1890s, this area became known as Japantown.

Despite their growing numbers, Chinese and Japanese Canadians were denied the vote in 1895. They couldn't hold public office or become lawyers, pharmacists, architects, chartered accountants or teachers. To practise in British Columbia, Japanese doctors and dentists had to obtain degrees from elsewhere in Canada, the U.S. or Japan, but still could not work in B.C. hospitals.

As more Asian immigrants arrived, opposition

against them grew. In 1907 angry whites smashed shop windows in Vancouver's Chinatown and the adjacent Powell Street area. The 1908 "Gentlemen's Agreement" with Japan restricted the number of male immigrants per year to four hundred; this number was reduced to one hundred and fifty in 1928.

World War I broke out in 1914. B.C. rejected the repeated enlistment efforts of about two hundred Japanese Canadian volunteers, so in 1916 they travelled to Alberta. There they joined Canadian army battalions and fought heroically in Europe. Surviving veterans were guaranteed the right to vote, but the promise wasn't honoured until 1931.

With so many people out of work during the Great Depression, resentment against visible minority immigrants only intensified. They frequently took unwanted jobs, at wages lower than white people would have received, and were then accused of stealing jobs from them. Even more disliked were immigrants who succeeded despite the many disadvantages they faced.

Pearl Harbor and After

After Japan bombed Pearl Harbor on December 7, 1941, Prime Minister Mackenzie King's government, encouraged by a few influential B.C. politicians, enacted a fateful series of measures that would displace the entire Japanese Canadian population on the west coast. The first took place on January 14, 1942, when

Ottawa invoked the War Measures Act to remove all "enemy aliens" from a so-called protected area. This same legislation had been used during World War I to relocate Ukrainian immigrants from their homes and put them in internment camps.

At first the Japanese community believed that only men who had not yet been naturalized (taken Canadian citizenship after being permanent residents) had to leave the 160-kilometre (100-mile) protected zone on the B.C. coast. The men were sent to primitive road camps in remote areas. But by February, Ottawa declared that *all* persons of Japanese racial origin — man, woman or child — had to evacuate the coast, including those who were naturalized or had been born in Canada. Families often had only a few hours to sort through and pack up a lifetime of possessions. Even those who had time to store their belongings eventually found that they had lost irreplaceable family heirlooms.

To cope with this massive evacuation, the B.C. Security Commission was formed in early March. Vancouver's Hastings Park became a "clearing centre" for people removed from the coast. Its exhibition buildings were converted into crude lodgings. Men were separated from their families and sent to road camps, while women and children were eventually shipped to detention centres in B.C.'s interior. Anyone objecting to the separation or resisting orders was shipped to remote prisoner-of-war camps in Petawawa and Angler in Ontario.

Mail was censored and a dusk to dawn curfew was imposed. Cars, cameras and radios had to be given to the Custodian of Enemy Alien Property. All property owned by persons of the Japanese race had to be turned over to the Custodian too.

The community was plunged into enormous turmoil, which intensified in the later months of 1942. Families were torn apart, education was disrupted, businesses were shut down and thriving neighbourhoods were uprooted and destroyed.

To avoid separation, some families from fishing or farming centres left the province altogether to work on sugar-beet farms in Alberta, Manitoba and Ontario. There they often endured back-breaking work and harsh living conditions. By October 1942 over twenty-two thousand Japanese Canadians had been forcibly removed from the B.C. coast. Of these, seventy-five percent were Canadian citizens (sixty percent born in Canada and the rest naturalized). This is known as "the first uprooting."

Detention Centres

Japanese Canadians were sent to "ghost towns" — old mining towns — in the B.C. interior, where local people hoped that an influx of newcomers would revive their flagging economies. Even so, there was considerable initial resistance by those afraid of the Japanese. Derelict buildings were roughly modified to provide housing, or crude cabins were built from green lumber that warped and let in the cold during the first hard winter. If accommodation wasn't ready when the evacuees arrived, they had to live in tents. For those used to the relative comforts of a big city, the lack of running water and electricity was extremely difficult.

Life in the internment camps was hardest for the *Issei*, or the first generation. They had left Japan with dreams of doing well in their adopted country and had laboured for years to become farmers, fishermen, shopkeepers or business owners. It was mostly the *Issei* who were affected in January 1943 when the Custodian of Enemy Alien Property disposed of Japanese Canadians' property without their consent. Land, buildings, vehicles and goods were sold at appallingly cheap prices. The money was used to pay for the auctioneers and realtors, as well as for storage and handling charges. Any cash remaining went towards the upkeep of the evacuees in the detention camps. Some people even received bills for storage of their confiscated goods! Japanese Canadians paid for their own internment, a condition prohibited for prisoners of war under the Geneva Convention of 1929.

But in spite of all these setbacks, the people persevered. Even though the B.C. government refused to educate the children of the evacuees, the community convinced the Security Commission to establish elementary schools in every centre. Because housing had to be built first, most schools opened late in 1942, and some only in April 1943. The person chosen to supervise this school system was the remarkable Hide Hyodo.

Only eighteen years old, she began teaching in 1926 at a public school in the village of Steveston, where many Japanese families lived. She could not even speak Japanese! Shortly afterward, the provincial government made it illegal for Japanese Canadians to obtain teaching certificates. Miss Hyodo was also the only woman among the four delegates chosen by the Japanese Canadian Citizens League to petition the federal government for the franchise in 1936.

Beginning in October 1942, she worked tirelessly from her base in New Denver. She personally selected and trained volunteer high-school students to teach in the ghost towns of the Slocan Valley as well as Tashme, located near Hope. Miss Hyodo visited each of the seven camps monthly to oversee the student teachers, and helped organize the first formal teacher training session in New Denver in the summer of 1943. Families were pleased that their children were receiving an education again, and school provided a welcome routine for those whose lives had been so drastically disrupted.

In the spring of 1943, families planted gardens in all the camps. People adapted to their new life and the *Nisei* came into their own. With better weather, the young people spent little time in the small and crowded cabins, enjoying instead their picturesque surroundings. Although some came from farms, fishing villages or other remote parts of the province and others from the big city of Vancouver, everyone was equal now. Freed from curfew, they could gather for social events, and community life began to thrive. Though some restrictions remained, the RCMP turned a blind eye when the Japanese fished, listened to radios and used cameras. All the prohibited items could be readily ordered by mail through the Eaton's catalogue!

By 1944 the evacuees were becoming restless. Many *Issei* discovered that their property had been sold without their consent, leaving them bitter and resentful. In August Mackenzie King declared: "It is a fact no person of Japanese race born in Canada has been charged with any act of sabotage or disloyalty during the years of war." But he then announced a program to disperse Japanese Canadians across Canada by separating the "disloyal" from the "loyal," and "repatriating" the disloyal to Japan, though many of these people had never been *in* Japan. Slowly realizing that their former homes were lost, Japanese Canadians began moving east to other provinces. This is the beginning of "the second uprooting."

In January 1945 those remaining in the camps

were forced to choose between repatriation to Japan or immediate relocation east of the Rockies. Over ten thousand people, uncertain of their future in other provinces — all of which had expressed their unwillingness to receive them — signed for repatriation. Many were Canadian-born children of the *Issei*, for whom repatriation really meant exile.

Also in January 1945, the Canadian government, under pressure from the British government, finally agreed to allow Japanese Canadians to enlist. About one hundred and fifty volunteered. Less than half saw active service before Japan surrendered in September, after the United States dropped atomic bombs on Hiroshima and Nagasaki in August.

After the War

When Japan was defeated, many of the Japanese Canadians who had signed for repatriation withdrew their signatures. In 1946 about four thousand were still deported. Half of these were Canadian-born and one-third of those were children under the age of sixteen.

When Japan surrendered in 1945, Japanese Americans could immediately return to their homes on the coast. The Canadian government did not allow Japanese Canadians to return to the coastal areas of British Columbia until nearly four years after the war ended. On April 1, 1949, all restrictions imposed under the War Measures Act were finally lifted. Japanese Canadians finally were given full citizenship rights, including the right to vote and the right to return to the west coast. But there was no home to return to. The Japanese Canadian community in B.C. no longer existed.

In the following years, the *Issei* were reluctant to talk about what had happened. They had lost everything they had worked for and could not get it back. Their children, the *Nisei*, also faced great difficulties in re-establishing their lives, but their relative youth, combined with hard work, enabled them to move on and eventually prosper. They too seldom spoke of the war years.

Redress and Restitution

Several decades passed before a sense of wartime grievances began to emerge with the redress movement of the 1980s. In January 1984 the National Association of Japanese Canadians sought an official acknowledgement of the injustices endured by the community. Over the next four years, rallies and meetings for this cause took place with support from churches, unions, multicultural groups and civil liberties associations.

On September 22, 1988, Prime Minister Brian Mulroney announced a Redress Settlement which acknowledged the offences against the Japanese Canadians during and after World War II. The settlement provided financial compensation and a review and amendment of the War Measures Act and relevant sections of the Charter of Rights and Freedoms, so that no Canadian would ever again be subjected to such injustice. The Japanese Canadian Redress Foundation was established to raise public awareness of the community's past experiences. Prime Minister Mulroney gave the following speech to the House of Commons on that historic day:

> *I know that I speak for Members on all sides of the House today in offering to Japanese Canadians the formal and sincere apology of this Parliament for those past injustices against them, against their families, and against their heritage, and our solemn commitment and undertaking to Canadians of every origin that such violations will never again in this country be countenanced or repeated.*

Glossary

arigatō gozaimasu: thank you very much

baachan: grandma

baka: fool, idiot

bentō: a packed lunch

bonsai: potted dwarf tree

furoshiki: a square cloth used for wrapping and carrying things

geechan: grandpa; see *jiichan*

hakujin: white person(s)

Hina Matsuri: Girls' Day (March 3)

Issei: first-generation Japanese person

Jan-Ken-Pon: rock, paper, scissors game

jiichan: from *ojiichan*; grandpa; see *geechan*

jūdō: a Japanese martial art

kimono: traditional Japanese costume for girls and women

manjū: sweet bean-paste bun

miso: soybean paste, a staple in Japanese cooking

mukashi, mukashi, ōmukashi: in ancient times, long, long ago

nihonjin: Japanese person(s)

Nisei: second-generation Japanese person

ocha: tea, usually green

ofurō: communal bathhouse

ohashi or *hashi*: chopsticks

ohayō: good morning

oishii: delicious, tasty

ojiisan: old man, usually a relative or family friend

okayu: a gruel made from leftover rice and water

okazu: an everyday main dish, usually with meat or fish and vegetables

omedetō gozaimasu: very best wishes

onigiri: rice ball(s)

origami: Japanese art of paper folding

ozōni: soup traditionally served on New Year's Day

sake: rice wine

sakura mochi: rice cake(s) wrapped in cherry-tree leaves, traditionally served on Girls' Day

sayonara: goodbye

senbei: rice crackers

shikata-ga-nai: it cannot be helped

sushi: vinegared rice

tadaima: I'm home

urusai: annoying, a nuisance

yancha: naughty, mischievous

yancha-bōzu: naughty boy

Spellings in the glossary are taken from Kenkyusha's New Japanese-English Dictionary. *The author always used the spelling "Geechan" when writing to her grandfather.*

MEMBERS OF THE 1941 TEAM BEFORE DISBANDING. Back (l to r): Yuki Uno, Eddie Nakamura, Nag Nishihara, Koei Mitsui, Kaz Suga. Front: Mike Maruno, Ken Kutsukake, George Shishido, Roy Yamamura, Tom Sawayama, Frank Shiraishi. Kneeling: Kiyoshi Suga

Watching the Asahi baseball team play "brain ball" was a common activity for Japanese Canadians before Canada declared war on Japan. Shown is the last Asahi team in 1941.

Girls' Day (Hina Matsuri) *dolls (shown on the shelf) were treasured heirlooms, passed down from mother to daughter.*

Japanese Canadians' fishing boats from as far north as Port Rupert were taken to the Annievile Dyke near Vancouver and held there. Many were so badly damaged that they sank.

NOTICE TO ALL JAPANESE PERSONS
AND PERSONS OF
JAPANESE RACIAL ORIGIN

TAKE NOTICE that under Orders Nos. 21, 22, 23 and 24 of the British Columbia Security Commission, the following areas were made prohibited areas to all persons of the Japanese race:—

LULU ISLAND
    (including Steveston)
SEA ISLAND
EBURNE
MARPOLE
DISTRICT OF
    QUEENSBOROUGH
CITY OF
    NEW WESTMINSTER

SAPPERTON
BURQUITLAM
PORT MOODY
IOCO
PORT COQUITLAM
MAILLARDVILLE
FRASER MILLS

AND FURTHER TAKE NOTICE that any person of the Japanese race found within any of the said prohibited areas without a written permit from the British Columbia Security Commission or the Royal Canadian Mounted Police shall be liable to the penalties provided under Order in Council P.C. 1665.

AUSTIN C. TAYLOR,
Chairman,
British Columbia Security Commission

This notice regarding "prohibited areas" appeared in the Vancouver Sun *and* Province *newspapers on June 19, 1942.*

The Bearer, whose photograph and specimen of signature appear hereon, has been duly registered in compliance with the provisions of Order-in-Council P. C. 117.

Vancouver
(Date) 5th March, 1941.

CANADIAN BORN

Issuing
Officer

INSPECTOR R.C.M.P.

All Japanese Canadians over the age of sixteen had to carry identity cards such as this one belonging to Kimiko Saito. The cards were stamped either "Canadian Born" or "Naturalized" and were signed by the RCMP.

After the Japanese air force bombed Pearl Harbor, distrust turned to fear. This Yellow Peril board game reflected the feelings that gripped the country.

Conditions at the remote road camps were often primitive.

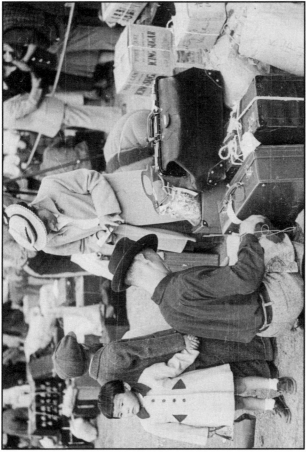

Families were allowed only limited luggage when being sent to the internment camps.

Japanese Canadians were forced to relocate to small "ghost towns" situated outside the protected area 100 miles (160 km) inland from the B.C. coast.

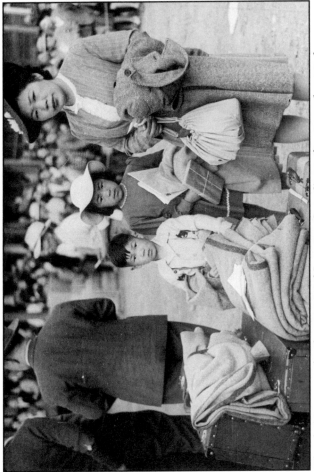

The clothing worn by the evacuated Japanese Canadians often turned out to be unsuitable once they reached the remote and isolated internment camps.

Though the scenery was beautiful, the rustic housing in New Denver proved challenging, particularly for those used to living in a city and having running water and electricity.

This family in the Lemon Creek internment camp was housed in a tarpaper shack. Primitive conditions and overcrowding were common in the camps.

Children sit around a campfire in New Denver in 1944. The boy on the far left is Tatsuo Sakamoto, who became a lieutenant-colonel in the Canadian Armed Forces. Another well-known Canadian who spent part of his childhood in the camps is David Suzuki.

These students are being taught by volunteer teacher Hideo Hiraki.

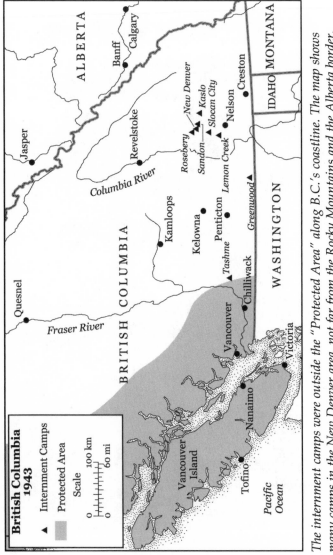

Quesnel

Fraser River

Jasper

BRITISH COLUMBIA

Revelstoke

Columbia River

ALBERTA

Banff

Calgary

New Denver
▲ *Kaslo*
Rosebery ▲ Slocan City
Sandon ▲
Nelson
Lemon Creek ▲
Creston

Kamloops

Kelowna
Penticton
Greenwood ▲

Tashme ▲

Chilliwack

WASHINGTON

IDAHO   MONTANA

Vancouver

Nanaimo

Vancouver
Island

Tofino

Victoria

*Pacific
Ocean*

*The internment camps were outside the "Protected Area" along B.C.'s coastline. The map shows
many camps in the New Denver area, not far from the Rocky Mountains and the Alberta border.*

204

Credits

Cover cameo (detail): *Fumiye Ohori, 1931 at age 13 years,* Japanese Canadian National Museum, 1931001.

Cover background (detail): *Japanese Evacuees Leaving Slocan Valley,* Japanese Canadian National Museum, Alex Eastwood Collection, 1994-69-4-29.

Page 192 (upper): *Last Vancouver Asahi team, 1941,* Japanese Canadian National Museum.

Page 192 (lower): *Hina Matsuri day,* courtesy of Molly Aihoshi.

Page 193: *Sailors aboard Japanese fishing boats in Fraser River,* Dominion Photo Co., Vancouver Public Library, 26951.

Page 194: *"Notice to All Japanese Persons and Persons of Japanese Racial Origin,"* signed by Austin C. Taylor, Chairman, British Columbia Security Commission, *Province* Newspaper, Vancouver Public Library, 12851.

Page 195 (upper): *Kimiko Saito's Registration Card, 1941* (Saito Family collection), JCNM, 2011.16.5.1.

Page 195 (lower): Yellow Peril board game, Collection of the Galt Museum & Archives, P19970041915.

Page 196: *Unidentified road camp,* University of British Columbia Library, Rare Books and Special Collections, Japanese Canadian Photograph Collection, 5.012.

Page 197: *Relocation of Japanese-Canadians to camps in the interior of British Columbia 1942-46,* Tak Toyota/Collections Canada, C-0470660.

Page 198: *Relocation of Japanese-Canadians to camps in the interior of British Columbia,* Tak Toyota/Collections Canada, C-046350.

Page 199: *Relocation of Japanese-Canadians to camps in the interior of British Columbia,* Collections Canada, PA-146355.

Page 200: Courtesy of Japanese Canadian Cultural Centre.

Page 201: Courtesy of Japanese Canadian Cultural Centre.

Page 202: Courtesy of Japanese Canadian Cultural Centre.

Page 203: Courtesy of Japanese Canadian Cultural Centre.

Page 204: Map by Paul Heersink/Paperglyphs.

The publisher wishes to thank Barbara Hehner for her attention to the factual details, and Dr. Michiko Midge Ayukawa, author of *Hiroshima Immigrants in Canada, 1891–1941,* for her historical expertise.

205

For my grandparents

About the Author

❧

Author Susan Aihoshi is a third-generation Japanese Canadian whose grandparents and parents were interned in the ghost town of New Denver in 1942. Her mother and several of Susan's aunts were volunteer teachers, while her father and her uncle repaired derelict buildings in Sandon before moving to New Denver. Susan's parents met in New Denver, then later came to Toronto, where they married.

One of Susan's lifelong goals has been to write a book. She says: "It has been a revelation exploring my own family's experience as people who lived through a major injustice and went on to thrive in spite of it. The highlight of my research was visiting New Denver for the first time and then touring the Nikkei Internment Memorial Centre, a National Historic Site. Visitors can enter some of the original cabins and view first-hand what life was like for the evacuees during the internment years. Writing this book has changed my understanding of my own history as a Japanese Canadian."

Susan worked for seventeen years at *Books in Canada*, a position that allowed her to meet many writers, journalists and editors. She later spent six years at Madison Press Books, where as managing editor she worked on a wide variety of children's books, including *To Be a Princess* and *New Dinos*. She is currently a freelance editor and writer.

Acknowledgments

This book would not have been possible without my mother, Molly Aihoshi, and her sister, Tomiko Kadota. Their childhood memories of 2321 Oxford Street, along with their later experiences in New Denver and Rosebery, provided rich material for Mary's diary.

Special thanks go to my uncle Barney Aihoshi and his wife Setty, and my aunt Alice Sakaguchi and her husband Herb for sharing their stories of those long ago years. I am indebted to Ina Boxeur for memories of Templeton Junior High and for providing me with invaluable copies of *TeeJay*, Templeton's student magazine from 1941 and 1942. Special thanks also to my mother's childhood friends and former Girl Guides, Margaret Lloyd and Michiko Kayama.

Thanks to Alfred and Lucie Iwasaki for their generous hospitality whenever I am in Vancouver. Nora Kaji, Stephen Kaji, Hannah Mizuno and Mary Rose MacLachan all helped me immeasurably. Emiko Mori and Toshiko Usami welcomed me into their homes and answered my questions. Thanks to Eve Baker for reading an early draft, and to Grace Gabber, Deanna Rudder and Basia Thompson for their helpful insights into friendship. My husband

Roger Stevens deserves acknowledgment as my intrepid driver in the wilds of Alberta and B.C.

For assistance with my research, I thank Catherine Miller Mort of Girl Guides of Canada and Sakaye Hashimoto of the Nikkei Internment Memorial Centre. Alexis Jensen and Linda Reid of the Japanese Canadian National Museum were extremely helpful in finding historical photos, as was Peter Wakayama of the Japanese Canadian Cultural Centre, Anne-Marie Metten of Kogawa House and Kevin MacLean of the Galt Museum & Archives. I also wish to extend my thanks to Dr. Michiko Midge Ayukawa, the historical consultant.

Finally, I am deeply grateful to Laurie Coulter for her advice and moral support, Hugh Brewster for his inspiration, Barbara Hehner for her fact-checking, and my patient and most wonderful editor, Sandra Bogart Johnston. *Arigatō gozaimasu!*

Library and Archives Canada Cataloguing in Publication

Aihoshi, Susan M.
Torn apart : the internment diary of Mary Kobayashi / Susan Aihoshi.

(Dear Canada)
ISBN 978-0-439-94660-5

1. World War, 1939-1945--Japanese Canadians--Juvenile fiction.
2. World War, 1939-1945--British Columbia--Juvenile fiction.
3. Japanese Canadians-- Evacuation and relocation, 1942-1945--Juvenile
fiction. 4. Japanese Canadians-- British Columbia--Juvenile fiction.
5. Epistolary fiction I. Title.
II. Series:
Dear Canada

PS8551.I52T67 2012   jC813'.54   C2011-905481-7

6 5 4 3 2 1   Printed in Canada 114   12 13 14 15 16

The display type was set in AlParmaPetit.
The text was set in Book Antiqua.

❧

First printing January 2012

Go to www.scholastic.ca/dearcanada for information on
the Dear Canada series – see inside the books, read an
excerpt or a review, post a review, and more.